THE DARK LANDS

ANGELBOUND ORIGINS BOOK 5

CHRISTINA BAUER

Brighton, MA 02135

www.monsterhousebooks.com

ISBN 9781945723452

For All Those Who Kick Ass, Take Names, And Read Books

A perky female voice sounds in my ear. "Great Scala, you're on in thirty seconds."

Blinking sleep out of my eyes, I snap up my head and look around. "What? Who? How?"

After a few seconds, I realize where I am. My husband Lincoln and I sit on the sidelines of the set for *Good Morning Purgatory,* the number one television show in my homeland. Our baby Maxon was up all night—and he's now with my parents—so I've had zero rest. I must've fallen asleep on Lincoln's shoulder. There's even a drool spot to prove it.

The perky girl in question looks in her early twenties. She's average height with olive skin, brown eyes, and long black hair. "I said, Great Scala, you're on in thirty seconds." Her gaze flicks to Lincoln. "And you too, Consort to the Great Scala."

Lincoln nods regally. My guy is also King of the Thrax and an expert demon killer, but my people only think of him as Consort to the Great Scala. He digs it, actually. Says it's better than getting fawned over as king.

"You know the drill?" asks the girl I've decided to name Perky.

I yawn. "A refresher would be great."

"You'll be interviewed by our new host. She'll ask you fun questions about your baby and that's it. There's no way she'll ambush you with some surprise just so she can get an exclusive."

"What a very specific thing for her *not* to do," says Lincoln dryly.

Perky keeps right on grinning. "Great, then you're all set. After your segment, we have on Cissy Frederickson, Purgatory's Senator for Diplomacy." Perky bobs on the balls of her feet. "I can't wait to meet her. What a natural for television! Have you ever seen her face to face?"

"Yes," I reply. "She's my best friend."

Perky laughs. "That's so funny."

I'd say, *no she's really my best friend*, but I've found it's not worth my breath. My people see Cissy as Mom's ally in the Senate. Guess that's the side effect of having your mother be Purgatory's President.

"Well, I'll leave you to it," says Perky. "Miss Frederickson is in make-up. Can't wait to introduce myself to the Senator. Wish me luck!" Perky steps away and as she leaves, I make note of her cat's tail. She's a quasi demon (part human and part demon) like me. All of us have tails and a power across one of the seven deadly sins. I'm guessing this girl's power is pride. She really seems pumped about her job. *Good for her.*

A voice sounds from the set. "And now, please welcome the Great Scala and her Consort." That would be Becky Tizzle and yes, that is her real name.

Lincoln stands and offers me his palm. "We're on."

I lace my fingers with his and together we enter the set. Immediately, I squint under the heavy lights. Massive cameras the size of water buffalo slowly roll across the floor, taking in me and Lincoln. For a moment, I picture how we must look to all the viewers out there in quasi land. Lincoln is tall and broad shoul-dered with sharp cheekbones, brown hair, and the mismatched eyes that mark him as a demon-fighting thrax. He's wearing a black suit today, which is his Consort look. *So handsome.* I'm in my form-fitting Scala robes, which are white and fall to my ankles. Other key points are my long red hair, big blue eyes, and curvy body. The viewers probably see exactly what they expect. It's not like Lincoln and I vary our Purgatory style much.

My tail pops up over my shoulder to wave at the camera because *of course it does. What a ham.* I'm part Furor demon, so I have demonic powers over both lust and wrath. My tail is long, black, covered in dragonscales, and all around badass.

Lincoln and I sit in the loveseat across from Becky's chair. For her part, Becky has short blonde hair, thick-rimmed glasses, and a peacock tail, which tells me her demonic power is pride; it's a popular sin with people who work in television. Today Becky wears a tweed suit and a predatory smile.

I recall Perky's not-a-warning.

Uh oh.

"Welcome, Great Scala and Consort," says Becky.

"Glad to be here," I offer.

Lincoln shoots a thumbs-up to the camera. Polls show quasis like it best when he sits there, looks handsome, and doesn't say much. I thought Lincoln might be offended, but he's turned it into a game. How long can he go without saying a word? Last interview, he got away with only saying *'hey nonny nonny'* and that's it. In case you're wondering, he was answering a question about the middle ages (his people are stuck in them) and I guess *'hey nonny nonny'* was a catchphrase back then.

"Let's start with a few questions about your baby," says Becky.

At the mention of the word *baby*, the studio audience lets out a long *ooh.* Everybody loves babies. I glance down at the television monitors by my feet. These things are out of camera range, but they've been placed so that Lincoln, Becky, and I can see the same things as the viewers at home. The picture of a cherub-like Maxon comes on the screen. My boy is all big eyes, chubby belly, and toothless smile.

"Isn't he adorable?" asks Becky to the audience.

More *oohs* follow, this time with a few *ahhs* thrown in. More photos go streaming by. In all of them, Lincoln and Maxon look adorable. I always have something stuck in my teeth or one eye closed. Whatever magic I have, it's not with the camera.

Even so, I settle into my loveseat and enjoy the picture show. Maybe this won't be an ambush interview. After all, how can things go downhill after Becky leads off with baby Maxon?

The camera cuts back to the studio. Becky starts in again. "We heard your parents, the President and First Man, have set up a baby room for little Maxon."

"That they have," I wave at the camera. "Hi, Mom and Dad! Thanks for watching Maxon today!"

"How old is he now?"

"Six months. But he's as large and smart as a toddler."

"You're the Great Scala, so Maxon's the Scala Heir, isn't that right?"

You think?

"Yes, I'm the Great Scala, the only being with the blood of an angel, demon, and human, in case any of your viewers missed it." *Not sure how that would happen, but this is Becky's show. I just answer questions.* "I'm also the only one who can move souls to Heaven or Hell. Maxon also has the blood of an angel, demon, and human, which makes him next in line. As the Scala Heir, my boy develops a little differently from other children."

"That is so precious," coos Becky. She adjusts her glasses and pulls up a clipboard from beside her chair. I've seen that *clipboard raising routine* before.

Danger sign. Ambush ahead.

"This just in," announces Becky. "We interviewed a new victim of the vicious criminal who's been terrorizing the after-realms. This fiend is as mean, slippery, and vicious as a snake, which is why he's called the Viper. Roll the tape, Fred."

On the screen by my feet, a video of an older gentleman

appears. He wears a too-large suit coat with thick glasses and a fedora. "Someone snuck up on me from behind," says the older guy slowly. "Knocked me right out. My demonic power used to be gluttony. Now, I don't want to eat anything. Doc says I'm traumatized."

The video of the older man vanishes. The cameras focus back on Becky.

"For months," says Becky. "The Viper has been stealing valuables and attacking the innocent. Victims are knocked out from behind and left weakened. I'm here to ask what every quasi in Purgatory wants to know." Becky focuses on me. "How will *you* stop the Viper?"

I tap my chest. "Me?"

"You're the Scala Mother to our people. The logic here is obvious."

Two things about Becky's last statement. One, the logic here is *not* obvious and two, I hate being called Scala Mother. *So creepy.*

"Not following you, Becky," I say.

"Let me try this another way," says Becky. "You *are* a supernatural being, right?"

"Sure."

"Roll the tape, Fred."

Another video appears on screen. It's the streets of downtown Purgatory City after I went into labor with Maxon. People are camped out on the asphalt with sleeping bags, candles, and signs. For days, my people blocked traffic while partaking of questionable substances. I quickly spot some of my least favorite placards.

Heal Yourself Great Scala
Bring Forth The Baby
Don't Die On Us

Becky raps on her clipboard with her knuckles. "Your followers held a vigil, asking you to have a healthy baby and not die. And that's exactly what you did, isn't it? That was a supernatural response to a quasi request. How is that different from what I just asked regarding the Viper?"

I shrug. "Having a baby is more of a natural woman thing, rather than any special powers related to magical crime solving."

"Oh, I'd say having a baby is magical." Becky raps on her clipboard again.

Crud. She's on a roll.

Lincoln leans forward, resting his elbows on his knees. I know that pose. *My guy is getting in the game. Yes.*

"You're leading up to something." As he speaks, Lincoln's voice turns low and packed with menace. "What have you found?"

True fact: when Lincoln asks a question this particular way, people always answer. It's the *king thing* he's got going.

"New information has come to my attention." Becky holds up her clipboard. "The Viper has somehow broken into the supernatural prison of none other than Lucifer." The studio audience gasps. "Once there, the Viper poisoned one of the guards. It won't be long before Lucifer escapes. Isn't that right?"

Lincoln and I share a confused look. "The Great Scala and I have received no such information. Are you certain it's valid?"

"We received this data from a ghoul named WKR-7," explains Becky. "He's supposed to be very reliable."

"Walker?" It's an effort not to screech the name. "You got this intel from Walker?"

"Why yes," answers Becky. "Have you heard of him?"

"He's my honorary older brother and Lincoln's best friend."

"Then you know this information is valid and the threat is real. Need I remind you why Lucifer was jailed? Roll it, Fred."

Again, fresh video shows on the screen. This time, angels in silver armor fly across a gray sky, their swords held high. These warriors swoop and dive over a retreating crowd of ghouls, quasis, and humans. Angels ruthlessly cut down the innocents. Blood is everywhere. Text at the bottom of the screen says 're-

enacted history' but that won't matter to most. The facts are true, even if the footage is faked up. Lucifer was a bloodthirsty maniac.

The video switches to show one angel close up. He has golden everything: hair, armor, and wings. *Lucifer.* He paces before a line of fresh angelic troops.

"My Brimstone Legion," declares Lucifer. "All was peaceful in the universe until the Almighty created ghouls, quasis, and humans. Then we were asked to help these lesser beings. I won't have it! Non-angelic life is worthless. Now take to the skies and destroy what should never have been created." The angels unfold their wings and rise up into the air. The video ends; the feed returns to the studio.

Becky rounds on me. "Now, what do you say? How will you save us when the Viper releases Lucifer?"

I have no idea what to say, but I do know what to think.

Fuuuuuuuuuuuuuuuck.

CHAPTER 2

There's a long moment where Becky's question seems to echo through the air. "How will you save us when the Viper releases Lucifer?" The studio audience waits breathlessly. Becky holds her clipboard so tightly, I'm shocked it doesn't snap.

All eyes are on me.

Thank goodness I spent my formative years sneaking out of ghoul-school. I have a deep reservoir of ways to leave sucky situations like this one. Lifting my wrist, I point to my non-existent watch. "Oh my, look at the time! Lincoln and I have to rush and investigate all this. It's been so nice seeing you, Becky. Let's do this again."

"But-but," Becky stutters. "You need to share your plan for taking down the Viper and saving us all from certain death at the hands of Lucifer. It was supposed to be a *Good Morning Purgatory* exclusive."

Lincoln wraps his arm around my shoulder and guides me to stand. "We'll get back to you."

What follows is a lot of pushing through crowds and avoiding of direct eye contact. At one point, I'm pretty sure that Perky grabs my wrist and tries to drag me back on camera. I might have tripped her with my tail.

Okay, I *totally* tripped her with my tail.

Finally, Lincoln and I make it into the limo we have waiting outside. For the record, I've never been happier for the invention of tinted windows. Once the door slams shut, I turn to Lincoln.

"What the Hell was that?" My mouth starts moving without too much guidance from my brain. This happens when I'm both sleep-deprived and freaked out. "My mother is the President of Purgatory. Saw her this morning. No warning about Lucifer. How does she *not* know the Viper's trying to free him? And my best friend Cissy is our Senator of Diplomacy. Hello? She has the best spy network in Purgatory and she was sitting in the same freaking building. Again, no intel. How is she not aware of this?"

Lincoln opens a water bottle and takes a slow sip. He won't reply. We both know I'm not done yet.

"And Becky says that the Viper somehow got into Lucifer's prison and poisoned a guard? And that happened *somehow*? Please! We both know how it works when Lucifer is involved. His magical crap turns up. It all started when Lucifer's Orb stopped me from sending souls to Heaven or Hell. Then Lucifer's Coin appeared. That thing could've opened a portal out of Hell and let Armageddon escape. Don't get me wrong—we took care of both situations—but that was a total pain in the ass." I lean back onto the leather couchie thing in the back of the limo. "Okay, I'm better now."

Lincoln raises his bottle. "Want some water?"

"Only if you run it over coffee grounds."

Lincoln presses the intercom button. "Please take us to Princeton Alley and drive through a Starbucks on the way."

Yes, even in Purgatory, we have Starbucks. Go us.

A note about Princeton Alley. In Purgatory, all the yuckiest places have the fanciest names. Princeton Alley is a little strip of nothing in downtown Purgatory City. Walker has a secret

Pulpitum transfer station hidden in there. I wasn't lying about having to jet off for a meeting. Lincoln and I are supposed to meet Walker in Princeton Alley and then visit some farm together. The details are a little sketchy, but that's how Walker rolls.

Which brings me back to Walker.

I try to muster up some of my previous freaky energy, but I'll need caffeine for that. "I forgot about Walker," I say in a super calm voice. "What's he doing tracking people who jail Lucifer, let alone giving that intel to Becky Tizzle?"

"We'll find out soon enough."

My eyes widen. "Becky Tizzle! We just speed-walked off her show." Leaning forward, I start fiddling with the controls of our in-limo television set. If being called Scala Mother is one of the nasty parts of my job, then in-limo TV is one of the sweetest. I flip the dial to *Good Morning Purgatory*. The cameras are focused on Cissy.

My best friend looks fabulous in her purple Senatorial robes. She's so camera ready, it isn't funny. Every time I see a replay of myself on TV, I have a chunk of hair sticking out of my head like an antennae. But Cissy looks amazing with her blonde ringlets hanging perfectly to her shoulders. Her golden retriever tail wags happily behind her. Cissy loves TV as much as the cameras adore Cissy.

"As Senator of Diplomacy, I have a unique view on Heaven, Hell, Purgatory, Antrum, and the Dark Lands."

Becky leans forward. "Tell us about the Viper's crimes in other parts of the after-realms."

Ugh. Becky is still riding the Viper train.

"Well." Cissy taps her cheek. "The Viper recently stole some ancient books from the Dark Lands. The Senatorial guard also reported some of their body armor went missing."

"We received that news months ago," says Becky. "Those crimes were early on in the Viper's career. The body armor was standard issue for the Senatorial guard. The books were far more interesting and rare. Show the covers, Fred." The screen fills with images of different covers. There's *Magic And Canopic Jars, Lucifer's Creations, Seraphim Secrets, Ghoul Portals,* and *Ancient Poisons.*

I'm so enthralled by the TV show, I completely miss our limo hitting the Starbucks drive-thru. But it did. Now Lincoln hands me a venti mocha.

Ahh, sweet caffeine, chocolate, and sugar. How I love you.

I return my focus to Cissy, Becky, and *Good Morning Purgatory.*

"Look at these books titles," says Becky. "Is it possible that ghouls have created an evil alliance with the angels?" If Becky's eyeballs were shotgun laser beams, Cissy would have red dots on her forehead.

Becky so thinks she has Cissy in her gun sights.

Not gonna happen.

"The purpose of shows like this one is to share hard information," says Cissy smoothly. "Not speculate and scare viewers."

Becky opens and closes her mouth. No words come out. *It's awesome.*

Back in the limo, I raise my fist. "That's it, Cissy!"

"She has such a gift with the camera," adds Lincoln.

"As fate would have it," continues Cissy, "I have something real to share with you about angels and ghouls." My bestie smiles sweetly. "Can you run the video I brought?"

"Of course," says Becky.

The television now plays video of a new statue being erected before a towering building made of glass. That structure is the Citadel where angels are trained in warfare. My father is the angel's General, so the Citadel is one his favorite spots in Heaven. The white marble statue depicts a tall ghoul in angel's robes. Under one arm, the ghoul carries a heavy book. His other hand is raised high, as if making a point to his audience.

I can't believe what I'm seeing. "That's Walker's brother!"

Lincoln grins. "Yes, that's Drayden for certain. I heard they were making a statue in his honor."

The television displays images of the towering statue, all from different angles. Cissy's voice sounds over the pictures. "Drayden was the first ghoul ever accepted into the Citadel for angelic warriors. And why? He wrote the definitive work on angelic flight and field strategy. His theories were used in the Battle of the Gates, when the archangel Xavier defeated Armageddon."

The camera cuts back to a close-up of Cissy. "This is what we should think of when we consider angels and ghouls. Not focus on the worst about our neighbors, but on the best of what we can all achieve."

I swear, I can hear thousands of quasis across Purgatory letting out a sigh at the end of that speech.

"Cissy is so going to be the next President of Purgatory," I say.

"Quite," agrees Lincoln. "And we've arrived at Princeton Alley."

I chug the rest of my mocha and grab the door handle. Lincoln doesn't move. "Are you still coming?"

Lincoln shakes his head. "I'd like to send out some messages; see what I can discover about these rumors regarding Lucifer. Once I'm done, I'll meet up with you and Walker as soon as possible. There's a Pulpitum station not far from the farm that we're touring."

"Great idea." Leaning over, I brush a gentle kiss across his lips. "See you soon."

With that, I return my attention to Princeton Alley and the mountain of secrets that always seem to follow my honorary older brother Walker.

One of these days, I'll get him to blab all of them.

CHAPTER 3

I slip out of the limo and into the worst-smelling place ever. Honestly, it's like a dumpster and a toilet got together and made an alley. The area is a thin break between two tall brick buildings. Any nearby windows are all boarded up. Graffiti covers almost every surface. The place looks deserted, but I know that's not true.

Walker steps out from the shadows.

"Greetings, Myla."

My honorary older brother looks as he always does: tall and pale in his long black ghoul robes. His hair is styled in a perma brush-cut with sideburns. It's the same look Walker had when his mortal form passed away in his mid-twenties.

"Hi, Walker." I step up and give him a peck on the cheek. "I saw the news about Drayden's statue. That's so great!" Growing up, Walker always talked about Drayden the smart, the strong, the noble. Most of Walker's afterlife has been spent trying to do what Drayden would have if he'd lived.

A pained look enters Walker's all-black eyes. "About that."

"What?"

Walker nervously twists a heavy ring on his finger. It's one that Drayden gave him and holds the image of a book carved in silver. Normally, Walker only fiddles with that ring only when he's really worried. *Huh.*

"Did you see our interview today with Becky Tizzle?" I ask.

Walker nods. "I didn't release any intel about Lucifer or the Viper." He twists the ring some more.

"So what do you know?" *Because I can tell you know something.*

"I share everything very soon," offers Walker. A bead of black sweat rolls down his cheek. "But we can't be late for this morning's meeting."

Walker looks so upset, I can't push him on this. *Yet.*

"That's fine," I say. "I'll wait."

A low hum fills the air. No mistaking that noise. It's the unmistakable sound of a ghoul portal. A moment later, a doorlike black opening appears behind Walker. This is the one perk of being a ghoul; you can create portals and move almost instantly between most parts of the after-realms.

Walker takes my hand and we step into the darkness. A moment later, we exit the portal and enter a strange landscape. Once we've marched out, the portal behind us disappears.

I scan my new surroundings. Gray clouds hang overhead. Neat rows of dirt stretch off in every direction, forming a countryside that reminds me of brown corduroy. The tangy scent of fresh earth fills the air.

"Damn," mumbles Walker. "I placed us too far from the farmhouse."

"You did?" My brows lift. Walker never makes mistakes with his ghoul portals.

"I don't trust my focus today," adds Walker. "No more portals. Do you mind if we approach the farmhouse the old fashioned way?"

"We can hoof it, no problem."

"Thank you."

Walker and I take off down a cobblestone path. We don't get

very far until a question appears in my mind. "What kind of farm is this, anyway?"

"I was afraid you'd ask me that."

My insides twist with foreboding. Something tells me I'm to receive the first in a long line of bad news from Walker.

Uh oh.

CHAPTER 4

*W*orms.

Why does it have to be worms?

Purgatory hosts farms for cows, puppies, chickens, and—my personal favorite—baby goats. So why am I trudging through Enmity Farms, my homeland's biggest producer of *worms* at this very moment?

Because my honorary older brother Walker asked me to.

Plus, Walker's a ghoul and his kind love worms. Long story.

It took me twenty minutes to get Walker to spill about the worm thing. And discovering our goal for the morning has been even harder. So far, here's what I know. We visit a farmhouse, meet some quasi demons and then … *something something something something.*

In other words, Walker's being very sketchypants about the whole deal, to which I say: *Meh.* I do tons of official visits. No doubt, this will be pretty standard stuff.

Shake hands.

Force smiles.

Pose for a group photo.

No biggie.

Then something unexpected happens. Walker lags behind me. The guy with mile-long legs and a constitution of iron actually limps along the cobblestone path.

Huh.

I pause.

Stare.

Do a double take.

Stare some more.

Nope, I'm not seeing things. Walker's limping. Even worse, the sharp angles of his face pull tight with pain.

A chill of dread crawls up my neck. Walker has the magical power to self-heal. As far as I know, only Walker and his fore-bear, the archangel Aquila, have this ability. *So why is Walker limping and in pain?* He recovers from almost any injury with lightning speed.

I adjust my pace so Walker and I step in sync once more. "What's wrong with your leg?"

Walker's shoulders tighten ever so slightly. He's bracing himself for something. That sets off my internal danger alarms because *nothing worries Walker.* In fact, I've seen my honorary older brother face down the dreaded Mordere, a demon that combines the worst of a humanoid vampire bat with the best in poisonous porcupine quill action. At a minimum, fighting a Mordere should cause a nervous twitch or two. But Walker? The guy didn't flinch. Then Mister Cool took that Mordere down in two minutes flat.

All of which adds up to one conclusion. Whatever's bothering Walker today, it's serious business.

"What happened to my leg indeed?" intones Walker at last. As always, his voice is deep and resonant. "That's not easy to answer."

My mind quickly sorts through recent Walker-related news. One item stands out in huge neon letters. "Mom says you had some trouble in downtown Purgatory. Is that when you got injured?"

For the record, I hate that Walker trucks around Purgatory without guards. Sure, the Viper is running around, but that's not all there is to worry about. My people hate ghouls. Walker's a great warrior—he even invented a new style of fighting called Ghoul Chi—but he's just one guy.

"When did your mother say such a thing?" asks Walker.

"This morning when I dropped off Maxon. Mom's super worried that you got targeted by the Viper."

Walker doesn't say anything for a long minute. He's definitely debating whether to finally open up. The question is, what will Walker choose? Will he blab or keep acting sketchy?

"How is your sweet baby boy?" asks Walker.

And I have my answer. That would be keep acting sketchy.

"Maxon is giggly. Adorable. Perfect." I wag my finger at him. "Stop trying to change the subject."

Walker shakes his head. "Your mother shouldn't worry about what happened. Many people have been targeted by the Viper."

"What? The Viper targeted you? How many times have you been hit?"

"Four or five. The Viper just likes to knock me out and move on. Doesn't steal any valuables. It's more an annoyance than anything."

I stop. "Walker, it's Myla here. Can you tell me what's happening? I know you want to."

Stepping in front of me, Walker grips my shoulders. His large, soulful, and all-black eyes lock onto my gaze. "I've been trying to tell you for a week," he says, his voice rasping with grief. "This is so hard."

Before a little chill had been working its way up my neck. Now that sensation transforms into a full-on body freeze of fear. "You're scaring me."

"It's been my privilege to help raise you," says Walker, his tone still rough. "I want you to know that."

I frown. "Still scaring me."

"I was born part archangel," continues Walker. He speaks with the careful rhythm of someone who's practiced this speech many times. "When I became a ghoul after death, it should've limited my afterlife. Ghouls don't attend Heaven's Citadel for warrior training. My older brother Drayden was the first ghoul ever accepted."

"Drayden was brilliant." This is my standard statement whenever Walker mentions his older brother. Which is a lot.

Walker's all-black eyes turn dreamy. "As a descendant of Aquila, Drayden received the gift of a magically enhanced intellect. He focused that gift on battle planning. My power is self healing." Walker rubs his injured leg. "And that's been failing lately."

"Becky talked about that on *Good Morning Purgatory*," I offer. "It's a side affect of being attacked by the Viper."

That dreamy look remains in Walker's eyes. *Not sure he heard me there.*

"After Drayden died, your father brought me to the Citadel council." Walker lifts his voice into a dead-on Dad impersonation. "'I'm the General of the Angelic Army,' your father said. 'This man is Drayden's brother. He gets trained.'"

"That sure sounds like Dad." When my father makes up his mind on something, you have two choices: get out of his way … or get out of his way, fast.

"Without your father's help, I'd never have become an angelic warrior. To this day, I live by the sacred values of his Angelic Army: honor, service, and sacrifice."

I can only repeat that last word. "Sacrifice?"

This time, Walker heard me clearly. He meets my gaze straight on. "Yes."

Oh, no.

"Look," I begin. "I've watched my share of movies on the Human Channel. No question what you're up to here. This is a *hero speech*. It happens right before the good guy does something like…" I wave my hands, trying to find the words. "I've got it." I snap my fingers. "Like fly his fighter jet slap-bang into an enemy battle cruiser. BOOM!" My pulse speeds. "Tell me I'm wrong."

A sad smile rounds Walker's mouth. "This is indeed a variety of *hero speech*."

Panic shoots down my spine. My mouth starts moving on its own. "No way. Nuh-uh. You're not flying your figurative fighter jet into someone else's battleship. That whole concept stops right now. Share what's up and spare no details. We'll figure something out." I point to the earth. "Your aircraft is grounded, buddy."

"Not this time." Walker's mouth thins to a determined line. "I require your assistance on something. After that, I must leave you." Then he adds a word that shatters my word.

"Forever."

CHAPTER 5

*W*alker and I stand on a cobblestone path leading toward the Enmity brothers' worm farm. That should be strange enough, but the day just moved from *slightly weird* to *I'll definitely need therapy after this* territory.

Because Walker, my only "family" member outside my parents, just told me that he's leaving. Forever.

Around me, the world takes on an unreal gleam. The gray sky, corduroy landscape, even Walker in his black ghoul robes … it all holds the wobbly look of a dream. Or in this case, a nightmare. It's an effort to force out my next words.

"Tell me what you need. If I can help you, I will."

Walker gives me a shaky grin. "You mentioned my brother Drayden."

"Yes, Cissy just did a segment on him during *Good Morning Purgatory*."

"Here's the thing." Walker straightens his shoulders. "Drayden's not dead."

"What? They showed his new memorial and everything."

"My brother is alive. All this time, he's been guarding Lucifer's prison in secret."

A sinking feeling creeps into my bones. "Becky said that one of Lucifer's guards had been poisoned."

"That was Drayden." Walker's deep voice cracks with grief. "He has less than a day left to live."

I pop my hands over my mouth. "Oh, Walker! That's terrible."

"Drayden has unique skills that enable him to guard Lucifer. My brother must be saved or Lucifer will break free. Only I can cure him. Today, I will depart to do just that. Once I go, there is no return."

"Whoa." I take a half-step backward. "That's a whole lot of confusing. What do you mean by *cure*, exactly? And why do you have to leave and never return? And who gave you this intel?"

"I can't answer all your questions. What I can share is this: The person who gave me the information about Drayden is another, ah, jailer for Lucifer."

Another, ah, jailer? Walker only stutters that way when he's holding back. I add *research sketchy Lucifer jailer* to my list of things to uncover later, right alongside *get definition of cure*.

"Also," adds Walker. "This fellow jailer believes that whoever broke in and hurt Drayden, they did so because they found a new item of Lucifer's."

"I knew it." I snap my fingers and point right at Walker's nose. "Back in the limo, I told Lincoln that this Lucifer situation included an archangel gadgets. What got loose now?"

"I don't know." Walker's gaze locks on the far-off farmhouse. "But I've heard the brothers who run this place are rather connected."

"They sure are; Cissy told me all about it. For months, her agents have tried getting info out of the Enmity brothers. But those dudes do *not* talk. If they won't open up to a fellow quasi, what makes you think they'll confide in a ghou..." I stop mid-word as the realization hits me. "They'll never talk to a ghoul. It's me who'll get them to blab."

Walker nods. "Word is, the Enmity brothers are very *religious*. They love their *Scala Mother*."

"Ick. I am *not* a religion. And I'm only mother to Maxon."

Walker's all black eyes fill with sympathy. "You know what I mean."

A sick taste fills my mouth. *I know what Walker means, all right.* Plenty of quasis worship me as their Scala Mother. It's more than a little disturbing. Some camp out at Pulpitum transfer stations, trying to glimpse me as I travel about. It's gotten so bad, we had to install extra guards—plus a 24-7 waiting limo—so I could move around without getting mobbed.

Speaking of being mobbed, there's no one around on the farm today. Which leads to another conclusion. "The Enmity brothers don't know I'm joining you, do they?"

Walker shakes his head. "This isn't an official visit. I thought surprise might help loosen their tongues." He tries to smile again. It only makes him look more miserable.

"Don't worry. I'll get them to blab about the Lucifer thingy." I scratch my cheek. "How else can I help?"

"I'd hoped you and Lincoln could be my back-up for saving Drayden. I only have a short time window in which to rescue him. If anything goes wrong, I need you and Lincoln to be available." Walker takes off his watch and offers it to me. "All you need to know is loaded on this device."

I take the watch from Walker's hand. A series of images appear on the small screen. There's a shield with a pattern of three feathers, a labyrinth map, and a massive gothic mansion surrounded by a funky gate. *Interesting.*

Walker speaks two words. "Alarm set."

With that, a flash of purple light bursts from the device, followed by a poof of violet smoke. I hold the watch away from me like it's infected with plague. I've seen this flash-poof scenario before. *A spell is at work.* And not just any magic, mind you. This watch just poofed out a purple spell from the House of Striga.

Thrax society is divided up into houses, and Striga has the best warlocks and witches around.

Still gripping the watch by its band, I let the device dangle from my fingertips. "What just happened here?"

"The watch is loaded with a few spells. I activated one to alert you in case anything goes wrong on my mission to save Drayden. And if things *do* go wrong, that device will give you a countdown until the poison kills Drayden. You must save him before then."

The world seems to pause as I soak in every aspect of my honorary brother, from his wide and capable hands to his large all-black eyes. He needs to save his Drayden. And to do that, Walker must go into hiding forever.

That can't be right.

Walker nods to the farmhouse. "We should head over."

My mind turns foggy. Things are happening so quickly and this is a huge decision. "Can't we wait a few minutes?" My voice comes out with a desperate edge, and I don't care. "Lincoln is meeting us here. Maybe he can help you plan."

"Trust me, I've looked at this from every angle. First, you must discover exactly what the dangerous object is from the Enmity brothers. Second, I'll save Drayden. Third, I go into hiding. If all proceeds according to schedule, then that watch will tell time *only*. But if anything goes ill, that device will start a countdown, as well as display all the data you need to help Drayden. Will you assist him? I need to hear you say the words."

I purse my lips and tilt my head, which is my classic thinking pose. Walker wants my help. *That's all I need to know, really. And there's no question in my mind; Lincoln will feel the same way, too.* Straightening my shoulders, I meet Walker's worried gaze straight on.

"I hereby make this solemn promise." I raise the watch by its band. "If a countdown appears on this thingy, then Lincoln and I will save Drayden before the time runs out. We'll also make sure you're safe and sound. And whatever's hurting you both? We will track that shit down and kick its ass. Hard."

Walker exhales. "That's more than I asked for but ... thank you. And I'm afraid some parts of saving Drayden may need your creative touch."

Meaning he doesn't know how to do it. "Bah. I'll figure it out." *Hopefully.*

"Thank you once again."

"I have conditions, though."

"Which are?"

"I fully expect you to be in touch from your *disappearing place.*" I make little air quotes with my fingers when I say the words *disappearing place.* "Maybe you can pick somewhere warm that Lincoln and I can visit, like a beach?"

The look on Walker's face turns unreadable. "I'm not going to a beach."

I tap the watch face. "Yet the details about your final location *are* in here somewhere."

"Only if things go wrong, Myla. Don't get any ideas."

"You know me." I shrug. "I have ideas."

"Please don't waste your time. There's no way to break the information locking spells loaded on that watch."

Bah. If Walker's hiding place is loaded in this watch, then I'll find him somehow. Besides, Walker's done sneaky stuff before and has had to go into hiding. He always turns up eventually. My honorary older brother is filled with big secrets and extra abilities. I don't put limits on the guy. Ever.

With my promise made, I wrap the massive watch around my wrist. The small square screen flashes.

10:21 a.m.

I hitch my thumb toward the farmhouse. "Let's do this."

"That's my Myla."

Walker and I resume our march along the path to Enmity Farms. This time, I take care to go slowly, considering how Walker's still limping. Soon the sight of his pained gait gets to me. I'm part Furor demon, which means I have powers over two mortal sins: lust and wrath. Just knowing that someone hurt Walker? My inner wrath demon seethes with white-hot fury.

Whoever hurt my honorary brother, they will pay.

Minutes later, the main house of Enmity Farms looms just ahead. Up close, the place looks like it fell out of the movie, *Gone With The Wind.* I'm talking pale wooden siding, tall white columns out front, wrap-around porch, the whole plantation named Tara dealy-yo-yo. Which is totally unusual for Purgatory. Most of our buildings are run-down piles of crapola.

The white mansion gleams pristinely in the morning light. While the front porch is empty, vague shapes shift behind the large bay windows. The Enmity brothers are most definitely at home.

Perfect.

I pause for a weapons check. Sure enough, my baculum rods are in their proper place, strapped into a holster at the base of my spine. The cool metal feels chilly against my fingertips.

Yes.

Since I'm part archangel, I can ignite baculum into any number of weapons made from angel fire. I glance over my shoulder at Walker.

"You got yours?" I ask.

There's no need to say anything more; Walker knows exactly what I'm talking about. After all, he's part archangel too. "I do."

"Good," I lower my voice to a hush. "Because if half the things I've heard about these brothers are true, we might be in for a fight."

The distinct sound of a throat clearing fills the air. Turning around, I face Purgatory Tara once more. Only now, the wide front porch is filled with seven stout men with red hair, full beards, and scorpion tails. And they way they're all glaring at Walker? Clearly, these quasis are not ghoul lovers. Even worse, the Enmity brothers' demonic power is wrath. It doesn't take them much to go from *zero* to *kill* zone.

A smile automatically curves my mouth. These days, I may be a queen, mother, and demi-goddess, but in my heart, I'm still an Arena fighter.

If these Enmity brothers want trouble, that's fine with me.

CHAPTER 6

The seven brothers keep glaring at Walker. All of them wear jeans, work boots, and green t-shirts with *Enmity Farms* written across their barrel chests in loopy cursive. They appear to be in their twenties. *Someone was a busy mom.* One brother—the only guy who's bald—steps forward. He points at Walker and speaks in a deep voice. "Ghouls aren't welcome here."

Rude.

After insulting Walker, the guy turns to me and grins. "Oh Scala Mother, you honor us with your unexpected presence."

Walker takes a half-step backward. "Perhaps it's best if I leave."

"Nope. Don't go anywhere." It doesn't shock me that the Enmity brothers want Walker gone. Most quasis hate ghouls. That said, Walker's on a time crunch. He'll get info fastest by staying here. I won't waste precious minutes because these new dudes are carrying old grudges.

Slapping on my best smile, I give a hearty wave. "How about a quick chat?" I focus mostly on the bald guy, since I'm guessing he runs the show.

Crickets.

Actually, crickets would suggest some kind of sound instead of the perfect silence that now surrounds us.

I force my smile to widen. "I said, how about we talk?"

The Enmity brothers keep right on glaring at Walker. Only now, their irises glow red with demonic energy. Combine those death stares with their green shirts, barrel chests, red beards, and matching tails, and it's like I'm trapped in an evil young Santa Claus convention.

Time to pull the deity card.

I stagger backward. "Wait a moment, I'm getting a message from the beyond." The Enmity brothers share a surprised look or two.

"Oh, Great Scala," says Walker in his most worshipful voice. "Are you receiving a message from your magical igni by chance?"

"Why, yes. I most certainly am."

"What an honor!" Walker grips his hands together below his chin. "Your igni are nothing less than magical bolts of power that move souls to Heaven or Hell. Pray tell, will they now grace us with visit?"

Walker's laying it on rather thick, considering how my igni rarely do anything I ask of them. That said, the Enmity brothers don't know igni are total flakes. At the moment, all those unfriendly worm farmers are slack-jawed with awe.

My igni simply must appear.

I can only hope they'll do as requested.

For once.

Closing my eyes, I sway from foot to foot. When I next speak, I take care to use a dreamy voice. "Yes, the igni doth speak to me." *Not sure if* doth *is a word, but I'm feeling it.*

"What do they say, Great Scala?" asks Walker breathlessly. "Is there a soul nearby that you should transport up to Heaven ... or must you open a *vast pit to Hell*?" Walker should do amateur theater. My honorary brother really sells the words *vast pit to Hell.*

"Huzzah!" I raise my arms. "The igni are on their way!"

In all honestly, there's a fifty-fifty chance the igni will appear, no matter how much I beg. But if they do materialize, it's always a crowd pleaser. And if they don't, I still have the *baculum and fighting* option.

Either way, it's really a win-win.

With my eyes still closed, I call out in my mind to my tiny supernatural buddies.

Come here, little ones. Make yourselves visible.

Instantly, the sounds of childlike laughter fill my head, a noise that only I can hear. *Excellent.* These are the voices of light igni, the small bolts of power that move souls to Heaven. Even better, they're responding right away. My lucky day. I should buy a lottery ticket or something.

Opening my eyes, I find a dozen small lighting bolts swimming in the air above my hands.

Good.

Considering how all the Enmity brothers are panting with amazement, it's clear the igni are visible to everyone.

Even better.

I tilt my right ear toward the igni, as if listening to their instructions. "What's that you say?" I nod as if their gibberish makes sense. Then I return my attention to the googly-eyed Enmity brothers. "The igni wish me to chat up your leader."

At this, the bald Enmity brother takes another step forward. Things are going so well, I could almost rub my palms together and say *mwah-hah-hah.* I don't, though. Now that I'm queen, I'm trying to be mature. That said, I'm still in my teen years, so I don't try too hard.

The bald Enmity dude waves in my direction. "I'm Travis. Folks call me Trav." He gestures to the nearby figures. "These here are my brothers Templeton, Tatum, Tyson, Terrell, Tripp, and Timon."

"Nice to meet you all."

They don't reply with words. *Nope.* Instead, the Enmity brothers only gape at me in awe. A few even have drool dripping down their chins.

Perfect.

"What do you need, Scala Mother?" asks Trav.

"Information. A magical item created by Lucifer has recently turned up. Any idea what it is?"

Trav folds his arms over his chest. "Can't tell you that."

I gesture toward the front door. "How about we go inside? It's more private."

"NO!" Trav's face reddens with a mixture of fear and rage. "We talk here."

Huh. That got a reaction and how. What's inside Purgatory Tara? I scan the windows with renewed interest. Figures still move behind the curtains. Maybe there are underworld criminals inside or something? Are the Enmity brothers hiding the Viper perhaps?

Note to self: come back later and check out the situation.

I hold my arms up, palms facing Trav. "No problem. We can talk outside. How about a little game of *fill in the blank*? The new object from Lucifer is a…" I roll my hand in circles, encouraging him to finish the sentence.

Trav shudders. "I shouldn't talk about this. People give us information because we *don't share it.*"

People like the Viper, no doubt. These guys suck.

"I respect that. You don't want to blab your secrets." Even so, what Trav *wants to do* and what I'll *force him into* are two different things. Dude just needs a little more inspiration.

It's igni time.

I cup my hand by my ear once more. "What's that you say, oh my igni? I should send this man to Hell?"

For the record, I won't send Trav to the fiery down under. *But I could.*

"No, not Hell!" Trav's bulky form trembles with fear. "Fine, I'll tell you. Word is, new battle armor has turned up."

I glance over to Walker. "Is that specific enough?"

"Not by a long shot," Walker retorts.

"*Battle armor* covers a lot of territory. How about a name?" I hitch my thumb toward my igni. "Last chance before I open the Hell pit."

If this were a cartoon, Trav's eyes would bug out at least a foot from his head. "Don't send me away. I'll talk!"

I set my fist on my hip. "Waiting."

"The armor is called Lucifer's Gauntlets, and that's all I know. Honestly."

I so don't believe him. That said, I'm not the one on a time crunch. I turn to Walker. "What do you say? Should we ask more questions?"

As a ghoul, Walker is already bloodless and pale. Now his skin turns such a pure shade of white, I worry that he'll pass out. "Not the Gauntlets."

My skin prickles over with gooseflesh. "What's the deal with Lucifer's Gauntlets?"

Walker scrubs his hand down his face. "The Gauntlets are metal gloves. They can pull out someone else's native powers. Then, they can place those abilities into a magical storage container or directly into another being. This is terrible."

I set my hand on my throat. "So someone could pull out my demonic wrath forever?"

"I'm afraid so," says Walker. His normally-low voice has turned especially deep. "Or pull out a ghoul's ability to portal."

My heart sinks. No question where this logic is going. When the Viper knocked out Walker, he put on those gauntlets, pulled out Walker's own ability to create portals, and then used Walker's very own power to sneak in and poison Drayden.

Damn, that's evil stuff.

My tail pokes my shoulder in a nervous rhythm. I pat the arrowhead end. "It's all right, boy. We'll never let anyone take our powers."

A low hum fills the air before a door-like black opening appears behind Walker. It's another ghoul portal.

My blood chills. "You're not taking off right this second, are you?"

"I have no choice," answers Walker. "Keep an eye on that watch. If there is no change after twenty four hours, then there's nothing more you need to do."

I try to nod, but my body won't comply. In fact, it's all I can do to stand rooted to the spot. *This moment, right here.* This could be the last time I see Walker. Part of me screams that I should have some awesome farewell speech handy. More of me just can't process what's happening.

Walker twists the ring from Drayden off his finger. With a trembling hand, he offers the precious band to me.

My eyes sting with held-in tears. "No Walker. That's from Drayden. You keep it."

Walker resets the ring on his finger. "Thank you, Myla." He gives me another sad smile.

With that, my honorary older brother turns about, steps through the portal, and disappears into darkness. Seconds later, the portal itself vanishes.

My heart feels wrenched from my body. I can't believe it.

Walker is gone.

CHAPTER 7

*O*n reflex, I set my palm over my new wristwatch. Walker said he'd hide forever, but the location is loaded on this watch. Suddenly, it's become my most important possession.

Trav speaks, breaking up my thoughts. "Oh, Scala Mother. May I give you a humble word of advice?"

"No."

That doesn't stop Trav from sharing, however. "Leave that ghoul alone. You're our sacred Scala Mother. Ghouls are evil. Befriending one risks your life. And if a foul ghoul gave you that very watch? Drop it in a ditch."

"Maybe you couldn't hear me before." I clear my throat and then speak in a super-loud voice. "NO ADVICE. And if you insult my friend again, we will have *trouble*." As I say the word *trouble*, I make my irises glow demon red.

Trav raises his hands like we're in a Western and I just pointed my six-shooter at his chest. "Apologies, Scala Mother. My only goal was to be helpful."

"Want to help? Tell me more about Lucifer's Gauntlets. You can't just know the name and that's it."

"I do know more." Trav sets his hand over his heart. "And I shall only tell you, my Scala Mother."

Fact: every time Trav says *Scala Mother*, I barf a little in the back of my throat.

"Here is what I know," continues Trav. "Rumor is, someone found Lucifer's Gauntlets. Started using them for thieving. Took books from the Dark Lands. Stole portal power from some ghouls. Been sneaking around all sorts of places, causing trouble."

"That's old news," I counter. "They were talking about it on *Good Morning Purgatory*. What I want to know if this. What does the Viper want with Lucifer?"

Trav shifts his weight from foot to foot. "I shouldn't say."

"Come on, you've told me so much already. And..." *How I hate myself for saying this.* "If you share what the Viper wants, I'll bless all of you, right now." I gesture to my igni, who are still floating around. "The igni will make it super sacred and everything."

Eew, eew, eew.

Trav perks up. "Really?"

"Really and for truly."

Although I might need to take a shower afterwards.

"Well, the most powerful person of all is—"

I hold up my hand, palm forward. "Don't say Armageddon."

"I wasn't going to. It's Lucifer. Word is, the Viper wants to steal Lucifer's powers. It would be the ultimate heist."

"Lucifer? LU-CI-FER."

"Yup. He's the most powerful of the archangels."

"But he's a psycho bunny. He'll never hand over his abilities. That's a good way to get dead."

"You asked what I know," says Trav. "Even though it puts me and my brothers at great risk, I told you everything."

Translation: the Enmity brothers know who the Viper is. Maybe the Viper visits this very farmhouse. I scan the windows once more. Nothing is visible. But is the Viper in there right now?

"Mind if I come inside?" I ask sweetly.

"No, just give us your blessing and be on your way."

"Sure I can't have like a quick tour?"

Trav puffs out his lower lip. "No question what you're think-ing. The Viper isn't any friend of ours. There's no evidence of the Viper inside the house either. I did what you asked. Now you need to keep your word." His tail arches over his shoulder.

He's ready to fight.

I narrow my eyes. There are two options here. One. I could fight these guys, burst down the door, and ransack their house. But that would be definitely bloody, possibly unwarranted, and absolutely end up as a story on *Good Morning Purgatory*. Plus, I have a rule—never attack unless physically provoked. Two. I could play nice, do the blessing thing, and then come back later and snoop. As an extra bonus, option two means I still keep friendly relations going with the Enmity brothers in case I need more intel.

Option two it is.

"No tour," I announce. "How about I give out the blessings instead?"

"Thank you, Scala Mother." Trav puffs out his chest. All the other brothers do the same. "We're ready."

After raising my arms, I realize one fact. I have no idea how to bless anyone. So I make stuff up. "By the power of igni and me, the Great Scala, I hereby bless the Enmity brothers and their farm." That feels a little light, so I keep going. "May your worms be wriggly and sell at great prices. May your tails ever arch and drip venom. And may you eventually see fit to give me a tour. And thusly, my blessing is over." *Again, not sure if* thusly *is a word, but whatever.* I twiddle my fingers at my igni. "Be gone."

In an act of stupendous compliance, my igni actually disappear.

Wow. Maybe I should buy two lottery tickets.

"Thank you for your blessing, Scala Mother." The other brothers murmur their appreciation as well.

"Glad you liked it." *Because I thought it sucked.*

Trav gives me a low bow before rounding on his brothers. "Come along. Let's allow the Great Scala to get on her way."

Trav stomps back into Purgatory Tara with his six brothers following along behind him. *Huh.* Surprising how they don't singing *Heigh Ho* with something about scorpion tails mixed into the lyrics. The door closes after them with a soft click.

Oh, well. At least, that's over with. Plus I happen to know that there's a Pulpitum transfer station not far from here. A short walk might clear my head.

Turning around, I scan the cobblestone path toward the main road. A little pang of excitement moves up my rib cage. It's goofy, but I'm hoping that Lincoln arrived while all the drama went down with Trav and Walker. All in all, it's been a pretty confusing day and I'd like to chat things through with my guy.

Yet there's no Lincoln. *Bleugh.*

With slow steps, I march down the cobblestone path. All the while, I try not to think about Walker.

No way will I contemplate how he always snuck me into Arena matches.

I refuse to obsess that he's not only a great warrior, but also a super talented artist. His drawings of demons belong in a gallery somewhere.

And I absolutely will not stew over this mysterious situation with Drayden and Lucifer's Gauntlets.

Nope.

Not going to worry.

This is me, happily marching along the path to the Pulpitum, not a care in the world. I have a chubby baby, loving husband, and nearly perfect kill record with demons. Why would I worry? My shoulders slump.

Fuuuuuuuuuuuck.

I already miss Walker so much, I could scream. Or punch someone.

Who am I kidding? It's punch someone.

~

Half an hour later, I march across an empty and muddy field. With every step, my sandals get stuck in the gunk. Each time I yank out my foot, there's this gross sucky-slurpy noise. *Ugh.*

The footwear side of this stroll is a disaster.

Now I could command my Scala robes to change shape. While slogging along, I've considered making them form snow shoes but a) I'm not sure that'll work on mud and b) if any locals take a picture, that'll definitely end up on *Good Morning, Purgatory.* Sure, the area looks deserted, but you never know.

Sucky-slurpy it is.

There's good news though. This mud march won't last much longer. I've almost reached my destination: a deserted grain bin at the field's center. This particular structure is a two-story affair that's made of corrugated metal. Overall, it reminds me of an empty tin can with a funnel-shaped top.

And it's never housed any grain.

Here's the deal. When Armageddon invaded Purgatory, I drove the King of Hell out with my igni. *Go me.* Expelling Armageddon was one thing, but getting rid of his demon army proved trickier. Those creeps found a ton of hidey holes and refused to vamoose. Not that I blame them. If I had to choose between Purgatory and Hell, I know where I'd set up camp.

Even so, the remnants of Armageddon's army couldn't just hang out. No, they had to do crap like chew people's faces off for fun. *Not okay.* Eventually, Mom put Dad in charge of a new Demonic Extermination League. About six months ago, my father constructed Pulpitum stations in key demon hot spots, like this one. Now thrax warriors can transport to trouble in within seconds, kill the big bads, and get home in time for … whatever thrax do for fun (there's no television involved, so I'm still not sure.)

I'm also unsure how this *backside of nowhere* farm country became a demonic danger zone, especially one serious enough to warrant Dad putting up a Pulpitum. But it did. Yet another reason to sneak back and check on those Enmity boys.

Stepping closer to the massive grain bin, I pause by the only door and pull on the handle. High-pitched metallic squeaks fill the air. The door swings open. Rows of cobwebs drift down from the threshold, reminding me of ghostly arms that reach for my throat. I shiver.

Wait a second.

Ghostly arms, cobwebs, and shivering?

All this stuff with Walker has me bummed out and wimpy. I'm Myla Lewis, and I can walk inside a creepy grain bin like a bitch.

So that's what I do.

Lifting my chin, I march inside the darkened space. Tin lanterns line the circular walls. The moment the door closes, those lamps come to life with angel fire.

I let out a shaky breath. *This is good.* The Pulpitum recognizes that I'm part archangel. I quickly scan the space for Lincoln. It's a long shot, but maybe he transported here and is just, you know, sitting alone in the dark for some reason.

Okay, I'm girl enough to admit when I'm being needy. I just lost my honorary brother, so I'm brainstorming crackpot scenarios where my husband waits for me in the dark. Fine. Color me clingy. I'll own that like a boss.

Even so, it all circles back to one fact. My guy isn't here. *Bleugh, part two.*

In the center of the ground sits a round metal platform. Once I announce myself aloud, that platform will activate. Afterward, I name my destination and the Pulpitum disc will speed me away.

Taking in a deep breath, I speak the particular phrase to start the process.

"This is Myla Lew—"

Boom! Boom! Boom!

The corrugated walls shake. Pounding sounds on the conical roof. The noise is so fierce, it reverberates through my chest. I suck in a shaky breath.

Silence follows.

"Hello?" I ask. "Is someone up there?"

More silence.

I tap my cheek and contemplate. Maybe some kind of animal caused the noise. Crazed baby goats could be leaping onto the roof. This space is really echo-y. That might explain everything.

On second thought, probably not.

Somebody's up there.

Knowing my life, it's someone awful.

Well, whoever's causing the ruckus, I've already had it with this day in general and this section of Purgatory in particular. My plan: activate this Pulpitum and haul my ass to a little place I like to call *not here.*

I take in another deep breath. "This is Myla Lewis, requesting the activa—"

BOOM! BOOM! BOOM!

This time, the ear-splitting pounding is followed by the screech of metal being torn apart. One moment, I'm standing in a darkened grain bin. The next second, the grain bin has a new skylight created by whoever's taken up residence on the roof. A figure leaps down through the new opening and lands before me. The scent of charcoal becomes overwhelming.

The good news is that the stranger is an angel.

The bad news is that she appears to be made from molten-freaking-lava. She's over six feet tall with long hair, even features, and medieval body armor. Really, she's your standard issue angelic warrior except for the full-on lava thing. Plus, based on the way she's fingering the hilt of her sword? She's not here to swap hair care tips or gossip about which lava angel guys are the hottest.

"I am Inferno," says lava angel chickie. "You may know me as the Champion of Lucifer's Brimstone Legion."

Now, only your top-notch big bads announce themselves and their titles. Since it looks like I'm not leaving any time soon, I might as well make the best of things and kick this chick's ass.

"Never heard of you," I say. "But you serve Lucifer, eh? How's that working out? Last I heard, the guy's in prison."

"You know nothing," snarls Inferno. "Lucifer is the father to all righteous warriors."

"Huh." A semi-wicked smile rounds my mouth. "Guess what? I'm Myla Lewis, the Great Scala and Queen of the Thrax. My father is none other than the archangel Xavier. Which means…" I tap my cheek dramatically. "My dad beat up your dad."

Inferno's entire body flares more brightly. Based on how she's also gritting her teeth, I guess I hit a nerve.

"Xavier is a liar," grumbles Inferno. "Lucifer is everything."

Growing up in Purgatory, I know one thing. We do not have lava angels flying around. *Nuh-uh.* My guess is that this chick's existence is related to none other than the Viper and his use of Lucifer's Gauntlets. There's one way to find out.

Lie my ass off.

"Congratulations!" I give her a golfer's clap. "I heard about the Viper getting Lucifer's Gauntlets."

Inferno purses her lips. "And?" The way she says that single word, it's clear that she really means: a*nd what else do you know?*

So I make more shit up.

"And then the Viper used Lucifer's Gauntlets to, uh, enhance you because you were, uh, dead as a doornail. Looking good, angel girl!"

Setting my fist on my hip, I do my best to look totally confident. Inside my soul is churning with the same question over and over.

Am I right? Am I right? Am I right?

"Indeed, I am thrilled to have life again thanks to the gauntlets."

Ha. Nailed it. She was totally dead and the gauntlets brought her back.

Inferno tosses her lava hair like she's in a shampoo commercial. "I shall use my powers to free Lucifer."

Now the idea of freeing Lucifer is no picnic, but I'll focus on that later. I'm getting valuable intel now.

"How about them gauntlets, eh? They are so good for, you know, grabbing magic, am I right? So interesting how that grabby stuff actually works. Like you put the magic in the container and it's in there. And then you put it in someone else and it's also in there. Personally, I like to keep a list of do's and don'ts. What are your favorites?"

Aaaaaaaand my cool-ass interrogation goes way off the rails. Will Inferno notice?

But Inferno doesn't catch on at all. In fact, I don't think she notices that I'm speaking anymore. Instead, her gaze is locked on my watch from Walker. Not liking the hungry gleam in her molten eyes.

"I know who gave you that device on your wrist," snarls Inferno. "It was Walker the ghoul. Renounce him and be cleansed."

I mock-sniff at my armpit. "Cleansed?"

"You will give me that device, of course."

"Ooooooooooh, by cleansing you mean you want my waaaaaaaaatch?" I make to take it off and then stop. "That would be no. And fuck you."

"Last chance, *Mother Scala*." The way she says *Mother Scala*, it's like I'm poo on her molten shoe.

"I'll give *you* one last chance. Leave through the door and live.

How's that for a deal?" Closing my eyes, I command the threads of my Scala robes to change into white body armor, complete with heavy boots.

Automatically changing into battle gear? Total job perk.

With my transformation complete, I focus on Inferno once more. "If this is you leaving, you suck at it."

"How dare you dismiss me? I came in good faith to issue a warning. Cut all ties to Walker. He is ours to hurt again."

Protective energy surges up my spine. "What do you mean, *again?*"

"Walker was attacked by the Viper, many times." Inferno smiles. Even her teeth glow molten red. "I serve the Viper. Once I am through with you, I shall find that ghoul and finish him off. Slowly."

"No one hurts my Walker." Inside my soul, my inner wrath demon awakens and damn, she is one pissed off entity. Energy and magic flow through my limbs, preparing me for battle. When I next speak to Inferno, I lower my voice to a tone I like to call *major menace.* "Oh, you're so going down. I don't care if you are a molten lava angel freak show." I crook my finger at her. "Come on. Make the first move."

Inferno unsheathes her sword, which also glows with molten flame. "As you command, Scala Mother."

She leaps for me and I smile.

This one's for Walker.

CHAPTER 8

*I*nferno lunges for me, her sword held high. There's a moment where the world seems to pause as my mind switches into what I call *battle mode*. Quick as lightning, I calculate possible attack trajectories and counter moves. I've never fought a lava angel before, so there's more guessing than usual. Who knows what this babe can do?

Inferno's sword glows red as she slices toward my neck. Although things are moving at normal speed, *battle mode* changes my perceptions. My heartbeat, Inferno's blade, or even the dust motes in the air ... it all slows.

Inferno's blade gets closer.

Closer.

Soon it's so near, the weapon warms my throat.

Time to act.

Channeling my demonic energy, I crouch down low. To a regular mortal, my motions would be too fast to follow. Let's hope the same is true for lava angels as well.

Sure enough, Inferno's blade swoops harmlessly over my head. *Ha!*

Without my neck to stop her momentum, Inferno twists her torso away from me. *Big mistake.* Pumping more demonic energy through my legs, I kick up into a high somersault. Since it's covered in dragonscales, my tail is already magma-friendly. While I spin over Inferno's head, my tail grabs her sword.

I land behind Inferno, who now whips around to face me. It's true that I just avoided being beheaded (*go me!*) but I'm now trapped in a *not so great* battle position. My back is to the wall while my gaze stays locked on Inferno. If I'm lucky, the door will be right behind me.

I'm not lucky. The only exit stands halfway across the room.

My mind races through battle options. I still have my baculum, but there isn't enough room for anything but a short sword or a dagger. Not a great choice. When it comes to hand-to-hand combat, Inferno has the advantage, what with her size and molten-ness. At least my tail swiped her sword.

Which gives me an idea.

"You're mine," growls Inferno.

I make a kissy face. "But we haven't even gone out to dinner." In my mind, I say something else.

Tail, do your thing.

At my command, my tail lifts Inferno's sword behind me. With a series of strategic slices, it cuts right through the metal wall. The steel crumples like tissue paper. I kick back with my left boot.

Slam!

Behind me, a large metal panel tumbles down, landing on the ground outside.

Helloooooo, exit.

Inferno scans my new door hole, frowns, and raises her fists. Up close, it's clear that Inferno's gauntlets are studded with small metal spikes. All of them are molten-red.

Yowch.

Crouching low, Inferno slowly sweeps her leg forward, trying to knock me over.

I don't think so.

Using my supernatural speed, I flip backward into an aerial. The motion sends me spinning out through my new door hole. A heartbeat later, I land just outside the grain bin. From my peripheral vision, I can tell that nothing's changed since I first arrived. Despite Inferno's arrival, the place is still deserted.

Inferno stomps out the same door hole, her right fist raised high. Once more, I wait until she's inches from my face before I move.

Oops.

As Inferno closes in, I try leaping out of the way. Trouble is, I forgot how sticky the ground is out here. My boots get caught in the gunk. I make it part-way out of the path of her strike.

Inferno misses my face, but her fist still rakes across my shoulder. Pain bursts down my arm.

With a gasp, I realize that Inferno's hit one, hurts like Hell and two, cut right through my Scala armor. It's not like I've done extensive tests to see what my magical robes can withstand, but I do wear these things a ton, even in battle. My robes have never so much as frayed before. Now my right shoulder looks like raw meat. Blood seeps across my chest and down my arm.

Did I mention how it hurts? It's like my entire right side of my body is on fire.

Behind me, my tail struggles to hold up Inferno's sword. Giving up, my tail tosses the weapon onto the nearby mud. From the corner of my eye, I notice the sword has changed from molten red to *I have no idea what that substance is.* The sword isn't metal, that's for sure. It's odd, but I'm not taking my focus off Inferno in order to get a closer look.

Inferno's fists are still raised high, but her gaze flickers between my mashed-up shoulder and the sword my tail tossed away. The question is plain on her face. *Which do I go after?*

Tough call, I guess.

Inferno goes for the sword. She tries to speed past me, her arms lifted in a defensive posture. Too bad she's wearing a ton of armor and the ground here is total mush. Her rush for the sword becomes a slow march across a muddy field.

My turn.

I race behind her. This time, I use the gucky ground to my advantage. At the last moment, I drop to my knees, using my momentum to slide right past Inferno. As I glide by her, my tail loops around Inferno's ankle. After that, I stand up and yank. Inferno topples onto her back. All around her, the mud sizzles from her lava body.

I'd do a happy dance of celebration, but Inferno now grips her sword once more. Although she's on her back, that doesn't mean Inferno can't hurt yours truly. Her blade glows molten red as it swoops toward my legs. Moving quickly, I remove my own baculum from their holster, ignite them into a long sword, and meet Inferno's strike. The two weapons spark as they collide. Turns out, my Scala armor may not stop Inferno, but angel fire works just fine.

Now that I have the offensive, I won't get it go.

"This is for Walker!" My tail spears straight through Inferno's right shoulder.

Inferno glances at the wound and laughs. I even can see how her tongue is molten as well as her teeth.

My blood chills. *Laughing at a skewered shoulder? Not what I expected.*

Inferno stands, a movement that forces my tail to rake down her torso. *Huh.* There are supposed to be a bunch of vital organs in that torso area, so you'd think Inferno would stop laughing at this point.

She doesn't.

That's when I realize the truth. Inferno is unlike any enemy I've fought before. I'm in deep trouble.

I try pulling my tail from Inferno's chest. It wobbles a little, but doesn't break free. Whatever Inferno's made of, that's some sticky stuff.

Inferno grabs the end of my tail and yanks. Now it's my turn to tumble onto my back. *Splat!* I career onto the mud. Inferno raises her armored boot and tramps on my arm. My Scala robes sizzle. Every bone in that limb explodes with pain.

"You should have promised to abandon Walker," says Inferno. With that, she stomps on my chest with her other boot. Agony radiates across my rib cage.

Turns out, it's hard to talk when someone is crushing your chest. "Never." Closing my eyes, I call out to my igni.

Little ones! Could use your help here!

No voices fill my mind, though. *Hells Bells.* Back when I was working over the Enmity brothers, my igni were all quick replies and supernatural light shows. And now that I'm being crushed by a psycho lava angel?

Nothing.

People talk about having their lives flash before their eyes, but it rarely happens to me. Heaven knows, I've been in my share of near-death experiences. This time is different. I picture Lincoln's mismatched eyes as he leans in for our first kiss. Maxon's infectious laughter as I tickle his plump little toes. And my parents slow dancing at my wedding reception. I've had an action-packed life, even if it ends up being short. Maybe now is my time.

Then again, maybe fuck that idea.

If I'm going to die, it won't be from a random lava angel.

My thoughts race through various attack scenarios. Somehow my tail is still stuck in this chick's rib cage.

Fine. I can work with that.

Closing my eyes, I summon my Scala robes to create cords between my torso and tail. Sure, I may not be strong enough to pull Inferno down, but in a pinch, my Scala robes can magically haul stuff. Instantly, thousands of white fibers reach up from my torso and loop around my tail. I order the threads to combine into thicker, muscle-strong ropes.

It's an effort to speak a single word. "Push!"

Both the ropes and my tail work to shove Inferno over. For a moment, her features fall slack with shock. Then Inferno tumbles onto her side. Once again, the mud hisses from her lava-ness.

I'm under no illusions here. Inferno won't stay down for long, so I summon my white Scala ropes to yank my tail free. Leveraging more of my supernatural power, they do just that. Next step in my battle plan: *get away from Inferno.*

Shifting, I try to stand. Pain spikes through my chest. It's all I can do to hobble onto my knees. With every inhale, my lungs gurgle. *Not good for my side.*

Before me, Inferno stands with ease.

"Walker is nothing," she says in a low voice. "Renounce him." Once again, she raises her sword, ready to strike.

"Never."

I pull on my powers of demonic wrath. Every inch of my body burns with agony. Even so, I must try and lunge out from under her slice.

Emphasis on the word *try.*

Inferno's sword swings toward me. I don't lunge so much as fall onto my back. It isn't far away enough; Inferno's long sword can still reach me. Once more, the blade seems to move in slow motion. Blood chills in my veins.

I wince, preparing for the slice.

It doesn't happen.

Looking up, I see that a rope made of angel fire now loops

around Inferno's wrist, holding back her assault. She roars with anger. "What is this?"

"Back off my wife," says a deadly voice.

At this point, I'm stuck in the mud with a broken arm, mushed-up rib cage, and a huge smile on my face.

Lincoln is here. And he's in full body armor. That's love.

I try to follow every step of the battle between Lincoln and Inferno. After all, I'm pretty sure this won't be the last time I encounter this lava angel. But paying attention isn't easy when you're thinking one thing over and over.

Ow, ow, ow.

Lincoln changes his baculum from a rope into a short sword. With a series of expert lunges, my guy gets few good swipes in on Inferno. As in, his blade goes straight through her.

For a moment, Inferno stands. Confusion radiates in her molten eyes. After that, Inferno topples over into two pieces.

That's what you call dead, right there.

Inferno may be down, but my guy keeps on hacking. I've never seen his face more intense or enraged. It's a little flattering, really.

"Hey!" I cry. "I think you..." *pant pant* "...got her."

After extinguishing his baculum, Lincoln races over to my side. He scans me with an expert eye. "Are you all right?"

"No," I say with my gurgly voice. "Lucas."

There's no need for me to say more. Lincoln knows precisely what I mean. I want to be healed by Lucas, the Earl of Striga. That will keep a low profile on my injuries. If word gets out that I'm hurt, my followers would have a psychic meltdown. *Good Morning Purgatory* would cover it non-stop for weeks.

"Understood," says Lincoln. His voice is all things soothing and strong.

I force out two more words. "Walker ... Danger."

When it comes to my honorary older brother, there's so much to tell Lincoln and not enough breath in my injured lungs.

Walker is my husband's best friend. Inferno promised to get him next. I simply *must* tell my guy what's happening.

"Someone's out to get Walker?"

"Yes." I try to force out more words, but I'm interrupted.

Inferno's body changes.

All thoughts of Walker evaporate as chunks of Inferno magically slide right back together, in the exact same way Lincoln cut her apart. Within seconds, she's reformed into a fully functioning Inferno.

That's unexpected.

I force out more words. "See that?"

Lincoln grips his baculum more tightly. "I do."

For a long moment, Inferno stands tall, staring right at me and Lincoln. Her magma sword gleams in her hand. My body freezes with a combination of concern and pain. If you can't slice up a lava angel, how do you kill it?

Inferno doesn't return for another attack however. Instead, she spreads her magma-bright wings and takes off into the sky. Within seconds, Inferno fades from view. *More unexpected stuff.* For a molten lava angel in heavy armor, she can sure haul ass in flight.

Lincoln resets his baculum into their holster and pulls me into his arms. That hurts like anything, so I suck in another agonized breath.

"I can help with the pain," says Lincoln. "And I'll get a search party going for Walker."

My guy reaches into a pocket on his body armor, pulling out what looks like a pen. Since the thing is purple, I know what it actually is: a magical item from the House of Striga—those thrax magically equip thrax for demon patrol. Mostly, Striga charms are enchanted to look like boring stuff so humans won't suspect anything. Normally, I don't toy around with healing magic because I rarely get a scratch. But now? Every nerve ending I've got is hurting.

That pen looks mighty nice.

Lincoln sets the tip against my neck. "You'll like the journey to Lucas better if you're unconscious."

I totally agree.

The pen pinches slightly against my skin. After that, everything goes blissfully dark.

CHAPTER 9

*W*hen I awaken, my head feels super-fuzzy. Even though my mind isn't clear, I can tell one thing.

I'm in the infamous Boudoir of Striga and no, I am not kidding.

Basically, this is a cavernous bedroom that an earlier Earl of Striga used for dalliances with his many mistresses. The chamber is all purple velvet everything—curtains, couches, and even tables —with the main attraction being a huge round bed, which is what I'm reclining on right now. Oh, and there's a fake closet across the room, which holds an unofficial Pulpitum platform. That's how Lincoln got us here from the grain bin.

Lincoln sits beside me on the mattress. Leaning over, he gently brushes a few strands of hair from my cheek. His skin is warm and firm, sending a shiver through my stomach. His mismatched eyes fill with light and love. "Hello, Myla."

I want to give him a proper greeting in return, but something else tumbles from my mouth. "My head's all weird."

"It's a side affect of the healing spells. You'll get clearer soon." Lincoln leans in to kiss my forehead. "How are you feeling?"

I pull in a few breaths. No gurgling noise. No hurt, either. My

Scala robes look perfect, too. I slip my hand under the enchanted fabric to test out my shoulder. My skin feels totally smooth—it's like Inferno never tenderized it. My wristwatch and arm seem fine as well, even though Inferno stomped on them both. It's not a lock that I'm totally healed, but things are looking up.

"Much better," I reply. "How long was I out?"

"Not too long. It isn't even noon yet."

"Wow. Lucas is good."

"He's become an expert over the years."

Some tumblers inside my brain start spinning again. They say the same thing, over and over.

Walker. Inferno. Walker. Inferno.

I sit upright. Every nerve ending in my body is suddenly alert. "Did you find Walker? Inferno said she was going to kidnap and hurt him."

"I sent out search parties for him. No one has seen Walker. If anything, Walker left word that he's leaves today on an extended vacation. What did he tell you? Are you supposed to see him again soon?"

"No." I hug my elbows. "He told me the opposite, actually. Walker told me he would go away forever." More of my foggy thoughts come into focus. "That's why he gave me this watch." I pull back the sleeve on my Scala robes and scan the watch face.

11:07 am.

I exhale. "Walker is safe. As long the watch only shows the time, Walker is fine."

Lincoln pulls on the neckline of his body armor. "I did uncover other information about Walker."

That sinking feeling returns to my bones. "What is it?"

"Walker has spent the last week sneaking in and out of Antrum. He's been visiting one of the lesser houses."

My eyes widen. "Let me guess. Does that house have a shield with three black feathers?"

"Yes. How did you know?"

"The crest appeared on Walker's watch." I tap my forehead as I try to remember the house's name. "Victoriana, that's it." I frown. "They're rather reclusive, aren't they?"

"Extremely. According to Lucas, the house has unique and magical ties to the Dark Lands. Some Victoriana gain magical abilities, but only when they set foot on certain secret stretches of ghoul homeland. Care to guess what's there?"

A prickle of recognition moves up my neck. "Lucifer's prison. It's in the Dark Lands."

Lincoln nods. "I've asked Lucas to find Cissy and meet us at your parent's place. There are so many pieces at work here. Camilla may know about the Viper. Xavier may know about Lucifer. You spoke to Walker. Everyone has a piece of the story."

"Agreed. Everyone must be in the same place so we can figure out a plan. That said, I can't wait. I have to tell you what happened with Walker and the worm farm."

Lincoln's gaze turns intense once more. "Go on."

"The guard who was poisoned by the Viper? Turns out, Walker says that was his brother Drayden."

Lincoln pales. "But Drayden's dead."

"No, Drayden has been alive all this time *and* guarding Lucifer. In less than twenty four hours, Drayden dies from the Viper's poison. Walker has a plan to cure his brother. Once Drayden's safe, Walker has to go into hiding for some reason."

"That's rather vague."

"You know Walker. Mister Secretive. If all goes well with Walker's plan, then this watch only tells the time. But if the rescue goes poorly, then this device shows a countdown."

"And secrets did Inferno share with you?"

I give Lincoln the side eye. "Who says Inferno spilled her guts?"

"Didn't she? I know your powers of persuasion."

"Okay, she totally blabbed. Turns out, the Viper used Lucifer's Gauntlets to raise Inferno from the dead. I'm not sure how she became molten, though. But who knows how the gauntlets really work?"

"True." Lincoln rubs his chin for a long moment, his eyes lost in thought. "We should head over to your parents. Are you feeling well enough to travel? The Pulpitum is behind the closet."

"Yes, I'm ready."

"I'll check if it's ready." Lincoln rises and steps towards the door.

Now, I must be 100% recovered because my attention is now locked on one fact: my husband is ripped. His black body armor shifts with all his muscly-muscles as he steps away. I have two demonic powers, lust and wrath. Right now, my inner lust demon is waking up to say *hey there!*

Lincoln pulls open the closet door (which is covered in more purple velvet, no less) and glances over his shoulder. "My eyes," he says with a wink. "Are up here."

"Oops?"

He crooks his finger at me. "Your Pulpitum is ready, Your Highness."

"Looking forward to it." Pulpitum travel is fun. I step across the room and meet Lincoln at the door.

He gestures to the closet interior. "After you."

I move to step inside, then pause. Somehow, leaving for my parents is like admitting this is really happening.

Walker is gone.

Moving closer, Lincoln gently sets his knuckle beneath my chin. Little by little, he guides my gaze to meet his. "Walker will be fine, Myla."

There's a second that lasts an eternity where our gazes lock. Energy zings between us. A simple thought echoes through my soul. *Lincoln is all things fierce and loving.* With him at my side, anything's possible.

Straightening my shoulders, I take Lincoln's hand. "Let's do this."

Lincoln brushes a gentle kiss across my lips. "Yes."

And that's all he needs to say, really. A thousand promises are layered into that simple word. *Yes*. It's an agreement to find Walker and end whatever is causing our dear friend pain.

With that, Lincoln and I stride into the Pulpitum closet and the next phase of our search for Walker.

We simply must succeed.

CHAPTER 10

*L*incoln and I squeeze inside the Pulpitum. The Boudoir of Striga is an unofficial transfer station, so this Pulpitum is a small circular disc set into the floor of an equally tiny closet.

Did I mention everything in here's still covered in velvet? *It is.*

Note to self: research Lucas's grandfather sometime. There's a story there.

After we step onto the disc, Lincoln sets his hands on my waist; I loop my arms around his neck. Our bodies meet in a sweet hug. Not only is it safer to travel this way, it's also recovery therapy. In any case, that's my story and I'm sticking to it.

"This is Lincoln Vidar Osric Aquilus, activating Pulpitum transfer station."

A young woman's voice fills the small room. "Your Highnesses. What a surprise."

"Hello, Juliana," calls Lincoln. My guy knows all the Pulpitum operators names because *of course he does.* Lincoln reads and remembers everything.

Juliana's voice lowers. "You're not in an official station. I didn't even know this place existed."

"That's funny," I lie. "It should read Arx Hall." That's our official royal residence, and it comes complete with a built-in Pulpitum. Which doesn't suck.

"It doesn't say Arx Hall though." Tapping sounds follow as Juliana fiddles with her controls. "The screen just reads *unknown*."

"Has Lucas come to talk to you?" asks Lincoln.

Here's the deal. Lucas is our secret weapon for sneaky Pulpitum travel. The Pulpitum *systems* are impervious, but the people? Not so much.

"The Earl has not visited me yet," says Juliana. "Is he really coming by?"

"Yes, he'll be there soon and fix everything." What I don't add is how Lucas will cast spells to wipe both her console and her memory.

Juliana exhales. "Excellent. Where would you like to go?"

"Pulpitum VII," replies Lincoln.

That's the main station in Purgatory. It's also an unavoidable time suck. Worshippers hang out around that Pulpitum 24-7, waiting for a glimpse of their Scala Mother and her handsome Consort. Some even make up little dolls that look like me. *It's way gross.* Plus, there's no way my boobs and butt are that big.

"Activating Pulpitum," I say. "In 3, 2, 1."

With a lurch, the platform speeds deep into the ground. I hold on tighter to Lincoln because factor number one, my inner lust demon enjoys it. But there's also factor number two, which is how dirt, magma, and geodes fly past us as we magically race underground. After my recent encounter with Inferno, I'll keep my distance from lava, thank you very much.

Another heaving motion rocks the platform as we reach Pulpitum VII. The station looks as it always does: a round Roman-style temple that's filled with nut jobs. Quasis are everywhere, but so is the Senatorial Guard, so Lincoln and I don't get mobbed.

Keeping a regiment at this Pulpitum was Cissy's boyfriend

Zeke's idea, since he runs Purgatory's Guards these days. Cissy was the one who decided to always have a limo waiting outside, just in case. Right now, they both seem like freaking geniuses. We'd never get to my parents' house if we had to deal with this crowd solo.

Even with the guards creating a makeshift path through the masses, there's no missing all the cries of *let me touch you, Scala Mother.* For the record, I have a strict *no touchie* policy. Other small groups sing versions of *Kumbaya* with messed-up lyrics—that's always a crowd favorite. Some older lady asks me to bless her toothbrush. And with that, I'm so done.

Get me out of here.

Normally, my parents' house is not my favorite hang out. Mom and Dad's place was built by ghouls back when they ran Purgatory, so the place is a cross between a Goth haunted house and a high-tech superstore. However, the way I'm feeling now?

Ghoul McMansion, here I come!

Even with the guards and limo, it's a lot of drama to get through the crowds and downtown traffic. In the end, it's 1:07 p.m. when Lincoln and I knock on my parents' front door. I know this because I've been obsessively checking Walker's watch. It's still only telling the time—no countdowns yet—so that's good. There's bad news as well, though. Lifting my arm, I show Lincoln the device.

"Does this watch face look cockeyed to you?" I ask for the twentieth time. "Inferno did stomp on the thing. I hope she didn't break it."

Lincoln sets his hand gently over my wrist, covering the watch. On the ride over, I kept revisiting about *telling the time* versus *giving a countdown.* Lincoln has been Captain Calm about the whole thing.

"It does look strange," says Lincoln soothingly. "However, there's nothing we can do until Cissy arrives."

"Right." Cissy is a techie, or what passes for one in Purgatory.

At this point, the front door opens a crack, showing a slice of my mother's face. Her pointer finger crosses her lips in the universal symbol for quiet. My eyes widen. In all the excitement about Walker, I forgot that it's naptime for Maxon.

I mirror the *shh* face back to my mother. "Is Maxon asleep?" I whisper.

Mom lifts her brows to make her *what are you, crazy?* face. Which makes sense. Maxon has never been a good sleeper. Someone's probably trying to get him to nap, and considering how Mom's answering the door in her Presidential purple skirt-suit, that someone is likely to be my father.

This ought to be good.

Lincoln and I tiptoe into the main foyer. Like most of the house, it's all gray wallpaper and black granite floors. One of these days, I'll sneak in here with yellow paint and go to town. The current ghoul-created décor is just bleak.

Once Lincoln and I are inside, Mom silently closes the front door behind us. Not for the first time, I'm struck by how she and I look exactly alike—auburn hair, amber skin, long black tail, lots of curves—only Mom has more wisdom lines and a streak of white hair at her temple. Love that hair streak, by the way. I am so rocking that look when I get older.

Now that I know Maxon's safe with my father, I return to my main obsession for the day.

"Mom, we have to tell you something." It's an effort to keep speaking in a whisper. "Lucas and Cissy are coming over. There's trouble with Walker."

Mom gently rests her hand on my shoulder. Suddenly, it strikes me that this touch is yet another in a long line of *calm down, Myla* style moves that I've been receiving lately. Normally, nothing gets me jittery. *As in zero.* If anything, I bypass whiny and go straight to all-out rage. What can I say? It works for me.

Not today.

Turns out, the very idea of losing Walker time-warps me back to the ripe old age of twelve, when the ghouls first chucked me onto the Arena floor to kill a demon. Back then, the pre-Presidential version of Mom sat in the front row, yelling *'baby don't diiiiiiiie!'* at the top of her lungs. All I wanted to do was cry until snot strings came out of my nose. Then I saw Walker hanging out in a nearby access tunnel. He shot me a hearty thumbs-up. The urge to weep went right out of me.

In that moment, I realized something. *Walker's right. I'm about to kick ass.* My inner wrath demon woke up; I made my first kill. Now, some deep part of my soul seems tied to Walker's strength.

How can anyone survive losing a brother?

Mom gives my shoulder a gentle squeeze, pulling me out of my thoughts. "Myla," she whispers. "Are the after-realms about to implode right this very second?"

"This very second?" I whisper back. "No."

"Good," replies Mom. She then glances meaningfully between me and Lincoln. "You two need to learn to pace yourself. Take time to savor beautiful moments. Trust me, you have one right now."

For the first time, I notice how Mom's carrying her heels in her left hand. In her stocking feet, she tiptoes away down an access hallway. I frown. This passage leads to my parents' offices, not Maxon's bedroom.

I shoot Lincoln a confused look. The question is there, although it's unasked: *why are we sneaking over to my parents' offices?*

In reply, Lincoln winks, takes my hand once more, and nods toward my mother's retreating form. He doesn't need to say his answer, either. I can guess his reply: *I have my suspicions but I won't tell you. Don't worry. This will be good.*

One thing I've learned about marriage. Silent communication is awesome.

Mom peeps through the doorway leading to Dad's office.

Lincoln and I steal up behind her. Fortunately, the angle of the threshold means that we can easily see Dad, but he can't see us.

What I witness in his office is so sweet, my eyes start to water.

My father has reorganized the room to have a military briefing. All his mismatched chairs face one wall. And on that wall, Dad has taped up a bunch of images cut from magazines or hand-drawn on sheets of notebook paper.

Maxon sits front and center, his pudgy little legs hanging off the edge of Dad's favorite suede chair. My son may only be six months old, but he's as large and smart as a toddler. Right now, Maxon wears nothing but his diaper and a goofy smile. He always reminds me of a cherub, what with his brown hair, huge eyes, and bow shaped mouth. Right now, Maxon looks especially angelic since he's out of his mind with joy. Why? In his left fist, my boy grips a full and peeled banana.

Uh-oh.

Clearly, my parents have no idea what kind of havoc my child can wreak with nothing but a raw banana. They're about to find out.

I nibble my thumbnail and consider the options. Sure, I could warn Mom about the impending banana-pocalypse. That said, wasn't she the one who said to savor the moment?

Well, I'll enjoy the Hell out of this.

My father paces a short line before Maxon. Dad wears a classic gray suit, blue tie, and starched white shirt. It sets off his cocoa-colored skin, brown hair, and bright blue eyes. Dad looks impeccable as he gestures to the various drawings on the wall.

Mom glances over her shoulder and winks. "Battle briefing," she whispers. "Fourth try."

I smile my face off. Dad is General of the Angelic Army. *This is getting waaaaaaay good.*

Nodding, Lincoln leans against the wall, a grin on his face to match Maxon's. My husband is definitely settling in for the show. I scooch closer to Lincoln; he wraps his hands around my waist.

What a moment indeed.

Damn, I wish we had a video camera. Or at least, one that didn't weigh a hundred pounds and need a fork lift to bring into the room.

Note to self: charm Cissy into getting us some decent tech to record our kid.

Pausing before Maxon, Xavier clasps his hands behind his back. "Now, soldiers, I mean, baby Maxon. Today's target is a nap." Dad turns to the wall of images. "Let's begin with some context. You may wonder—why do we have naptime?" Dad points to a taped-up picture of me and Lincoln. "You must rest so you can grow up healthy and strong like your parents. Do we understand each other?"

After jamming banana into his mouth, my son then sets the half-eaten remainder atop dad's favorite—and very expensive— suede chair. Having set aside his snack, Maxon slides off the chair and toddles over to my father. His little voice rings out. "Pop Pops."

My father's eyes glisten. "Oh, Maxon."

Maxon lumbers up to Dad. My little boy raises his arms as if asking to be carried, but I've seen this move before. Maxon does not want to be picked up. *Nope.*

Instead, my boy wipes off his banana-covered hands on Xavier's new Armani suit pants. It's a really good hit, too: mid- thigh right down to his knees. That crap won't come out. I've tried.

Le sigh. I've lost three outfits that way myself.

His work done, Maxon then toddles back to his chair. Leaning over the cushion, my boy tries hauling himself back up to sitting. That doesn't happen. Maxon only manages to grind more banana into Dad's custom-made furniture.

Lincoln and I share a sly smile. *We lost pricey chairs this way, too.*

Sighing, Dad scoops up Maxon and resets him on the chair.

With his little soldier back in place, Dad returns to pointing at the wall.

"Now," announces my father. "Let's review our plan of attack. First, we'll finish our snack. That would be your banana."

Maxon mushes some of said banana into his ear. "Pop Pops."

"Second, we'll read a book." Turning away from Maxon, Dad points to various hand-dawn book covers taped to the wall. Our choices today are *Goodnight Moon* or *Why We Poop*. But our reading selection doesn't need to be finalized at this time. That can be a field call. Are you still with me, Maxon?"

Dad turns back around. Maxon is now smooshing banana into his hair. And his diaper. And more deeply into the expensive chair.

Guilt finally gets the better of me. I tap Mom on the shoulder. "Sorry about your chair."

Mom rolls her eyes. "Are you kidding?" she whispers. "I love this."

Back at the briefing, Dad points to a cutout image of a rocking chair. "After we accomplish book time, you and I will rock while singing a song. This can be *The Battle Hymn Of The Republic* or *Row, Row, Row, Your Boat*. I don't know other tunes. Although…" Dad taps his chin for a moment. "I do know *Rock-A-Bye Baby*. Maybe that's been the missing part of our plan." Pulling a pen from an inner pocket of his suit coat, Dad adds the words *Rock-A-Bye Baby* onto the sheet with other songs.

While my father's scribbling away, Maxon slides off the chair yet again. This time, he toddles out a side door. My son hasn't noticed me, Lincoln, or Mom yet. I figure I've got about twenty seconds before Lincoln or I need to chase after Maxon. My son has a gift for destroying things.

Dad finishes his writing. "Fourth and finally, you will go to sleep. Do we all understand the plan?" Dad turns around, but Maxon is gone. My father scans the room and his gaze lands on me. His face brightens into a white-toothed smile. "Myla! Lincoln!"

I give him a little wave. "Hi, Dad!"

Maxon now toddle-runs back into the room. "No seepie, no seepie." To translate from Maxon-speak, that means *no sleeping, no sleeping.* The phrase is really cute until it's three o'clock in the morning.

The doorbell rings. Mom slips on her heels. "That must be Cissy and Lucas." She steps off to answer the door.

Maxon runs around in a small circle, continuing his chant. "No seepie, no seepie."

Dad rakes his hands through his hair. "Who am I kidding?" He slouches onto one of the nearby, banana-free chairs. "This is the fifth suit I've changed into today. The others got whacked with chocolate, yogurt, applesauce, and sharpie." Dad gestures toward the wall. "My briefings are a failure. I have no idea how to raise a child."

When you have a badass archangel general for a father, it's more than a little endearing when he admits he can't do something. I slip into the open briefing seat beside my father's (also banana free).

"You'll get it," I say. "Maxon's a little too young for the soldier routine, but you'll figure it out."

My father gestures between me and Lincoln. "You both seem to know what to do."

"I'm glad we appear competent," says Lincoln. "In reality, Myla and I are making it up as we go."

Dad sits up straighter. "Really?"

"Oh yeah." I shrug. "We tried baby books and stuff, but there's no book for Maxon."

Dad rubs his forehead slowly. "So, you got into the field and improvised. I've had missions like those."

"That's the idea," says Lincoln.

Maxon stops running in a circle to plunk onto the floor. *This is our cue to step in.* I give Dad a reassuring smile. "For now, why don't Lincoln and I put Maxon down for his nap?"

"And maybe give him a quick bath," adds Lincoln.

Dad brightens. "That sounds like a great idea. I'll put on another suit."

Twenty minutes and one bath later, Lincoln and I are in the baby room that Mom and Dad set up for Maxon. Our child appears absolutely manic with alertness as he grips one edge of his crib and jumps in time with his favorite chant.

"No seepie! No seepie!"

"How long do you give him?" I ask.

Lincoln purses his lips. "About 47 seconds."

Maxon stops jumping and reaches for me. "Momma boo."

In Maxon-speak, *boo* stands for beautiful. *Momma boo* means *my mommy is beautiful.* That is so freaking adorable, I think one of my ovaries just exploded.

Maxon turns to Lincoln. "Daddy boo."

Lincoln pulls me against his side. I lean my head against my husband's shoulder. Mom is right; we need to savor these moments.

"Maxon boo," says Lincoln in a gentle voice.

Aaaaaaaaaaaaaand I just ovulated again.

Gripping the crib once more, Maxon resumes his baby Cirque Du Baby performance. "No seepie! No seepie! No—"

And with that, my kid falls over into a dead sleep. *Beautiful.* In fact, the moment is so lovely, I can't imagine anything but good stuff happening from now on.

"You know what?" I ask.

Lincoln kisses the top of my head. "Do tell."

"By now, I figure Walker has already saved Drayden. Plus, I bet Walker has those magical gauntlets in his possession and has gone off to his so-called disappearing place. But now Lucas and Cissy will pull every last bit of information out of my watch. We'll find out where Walker is hiding. Everything will be fine."

Lincoln kisses the top of my head once more. "I bet you're right."

Purple light pulses from my watch. This is no normal tech light, either: it's bright enough to make me wince. A small poof of violet smoke follows. The mini cloud twinkles with supernatural light as it wafts up from my wrist. No question about it.

My watch just launched another magic spell.

Please, don't let it be the countdown.

It takes a major force of will, but I make myself lift my arm and examine the watch face. Sure enough, the time is gone. Instead, new letters and numbers appear on the device.

Twenty one hours, fifty-nine minutes, twenty-two seconds.

The countdown has begun.

CHAPTER 11

a few minutes later, Lincoln and I step into my parents' kitchen. The room is wall-to-wall gadgets and stainless steel. Like I said, ghouls love technology. Everyone's seated around our long table, including Mom, Dad, Lucas, and Cissy. My bestie is still in her Senatorial robes; we must have pulled her out of an official function. Lucas is in his long wizard robes. He's an older dude with olive skin and long gray dreads.

Lincoln and I say our hellos—including an extra-long hug for Ciss—and then we take our seats at the metal table. A long pause follows. For a second, it's like I've time-warped back to the Arena again. I'm twelve and frightened. Then I picture my honorary older brother shooting me that encouraging thumbs-up. Maybe I can't save Walker and Drayden, but I *can* keep trying.

I take in a calming breath. "Hey, guys." Ever since the Boudoir of Striga, I'd been thinking about how to organize this talk. "I'd like to start things off." I scan the room. Everyone gazes toward me with expectant faces.

Guess that means *it's all yours, Myla*.

"Here are the facts," I begin. "Walker's brother, Drayden is at risk."

My father leans back in his chair. Every line of his face is etched with shock. "Walker's brother is alive?"

I nod. "Walker only found out about Drayden a few days ago. Since then, Walker's created a plan to save his brother. If the rescue didn't work, then *this* watch..." I tap the device on my wrist "...would start a countdown." Raising my arm, I show off the watch face. The temperature seems to drop twenty degrees as they read the little screen.

Twenty hours, forty minutes, fifty seconds.

Silence descends. The air turns heavy with worry.

"Here's the deal," I explain. "I promised Walker that Lincoln and I would help if worse came to worst and the countdown started. Well, time is now ticking. Both Walker and Drayden need our help. Is everyone in?"

A chorus of yes-es sounds around the table. *Excellent.*

"In that case," I continue. "Our best bet is to find Drayden before the countdown ends. I'm thinking that wherever Drayden is, Walker can't be far. Each person here has a little piece of the story. Let's start with the watch. It might have gotten brok—"

My thoughts shatter as an igni music festival erupts inside my head. This isn't a cool rock concert, either. The dark igni are now in my brain, giving off a chorus of screechy feedback. Within the noise, I make out some words.

Prison.

Lucifer.

History.

I throw up my hands. "Quiet down, guys. You want the history of Lucifer. I got it. Now buzz off." And the igni actually leave. Where was this support when I was getting crushed by Inferno? No idea.

Lincoln sets his hand gently on my shoulder. "Another message from your igni?"

"Yup, it seems they have their own ideas about our conversation." I pull on my ears, as if that will somehow let the memory of the dark igni noise ooze out of my head. "Dad, can you start things off by giving us a history of Lucifer? The igni especially want us to know about his imprisonment."

My father fidgets in his chair. "If they insist."

"Believe me," I counter. "They do." In a show of support, my tail pops up over my shoulder. The arrowhead bobs up and down, which is its way of saying *yes*. I pat the end. "Thanks, boy."

Dad straightens the lapels of his suit. "Luce and I were close for ages. Then the Almighty created new forms of life, namely humans, quasis, thrax, and ghouls. All angels were instructed to help these new beings. Luce refused. He saw any non-angel as an abomination and ..." Dad lowers his head. "Luce refused to—as he put it—degrade himself. I can only imagine how that sounds."

Mom leans forward until her gaze catches with Dad's. "Lucifer's opinions are not yours. We all know this."

"Thank you, Cam." My parents exchange a small smile before Dad continues. "Luce was a good man before hatred ate him up inside. Even worse, Luce spread his rage and recruited other angels to his cause. Together, they called themselves the Brimstone Legion and began a holy way against all non-angels." My father sets his palms flat on the tabletop. Even from a distance, I can see how his hands are shaking. "Countless innocents were killed."

Another long stretch of quiet follows. Dad's shaking worsens. *My poor father.* Clearly, Dad's having a hard time with this story, so I give him a small prompt. "I think I know what happens next," I offer. "You and the archangels put Lucifer into prison."

"That's the story," explains my father. "The truth is more complex. We archangels tried to kill Luce many times. For archangels, we can issue a formal challenge for a one-to-one duel."

My father doesn't talk about Lucifer, but archangel challenges are another matter. They're conducted with specific rules of honor, including a mutual spell to ensure no one cheats. The battle can be to the death or to decide a dispute. Either way, the results are binding.

"We engaged Lucifer in challenge after challenge. Each time, the stakes were the same. If we won, Lucifer would disband his Brimstone Legion for a hundred years. If Lucifer won, we would allow his legion to *cleanse the world* for a hundred years." Dad's eyes fill with sorrow. "There are eight of us outside of Lucifer. Eight times we tried to defeat him. Eight times we failed. And that meant nearly a millennium of carnage."

"Luce was our king and trained us all," continues my father. "He knew our every move before we could make it. Defeating us was all too easy for him. Still, the bloodshed had to stop. In the end, I was forced to rely on subterfuge."

A memory appears. I picture the pure loathing on Inferno's face as she called my father a liar. Perhaps this is what she meant. If so, I don't consider that lying so much as stopping innocents from getting killed. *Stupid Inferno.*

Mom sets her hand atop Dad's. "I can tell this part if you like, Xav."

"No, I want everyone to hear this from me directly, especially Myla." Dad raises his chin. "Luce believed that I would never lie to him, so I used that faith to our advantage. I issued a challenge to Lucifer. One more duel, just him and me, and to the death. We would meet in the Dark Lands. But I never left for the battle. The nine seraphim went instead."

Cissy tilts her head, making her blonde ringlets bounce. "I don't know much about seraphim."

"You're not alone," I add.

"They're mages and high-level angels," explains Lincoln. "One of our thrax houses is dedicated to their memory." He gives me a pointed look that says: *guess which one.*

I meet his gaze and nod. *Victoriana, aka the one Walker was sneaking off to visit.*

"There were nine seraphim," continues Dad. "Just as there are nine archangels. Lucifer went to the battlefield, just as we agreed. He also brought his Brimstone Legion along so they could witness his final victory. So it became Luce and his Brimstone Legion against nine seraphim. Luce still thought it was a battle worth having. You see, only a full blooded archangel can kill another archangel."

Dad takes in a shaky breath. "Yet the seraphim's plan wasn't to kill Lucifer. Instead those angelic mages cast a spell so strong, their magic killed the entire Brimstone Legion as well as the seraphim themselves."

"Ah, I understand why they perished," says Lucas. "Truly great magic always requires a sacrifice to match."

"Yes," says Dad. "Through their deaths, they created spell that destroyed the entire Brimstone Legion while locking Luce away forever."

Silence follows. None of us seem to breathe. *What a story*. At last, my father speaks again.

"At my request, the specifics of Luce's final prison were hidden from myself and the other archangels. We don't even know what spells the seraphim cast in order to kill the legion and imprison Luce. You see, strange as it may seem, all of us still love Luce in our own way. If we knew where and how he was imprisoned, we might eventually give into the temptation to see him." Dad chuckles, but there's no humor in it. "Luce is so persuasive, he could talk the cold off snow. It's still a good thing I don't know where he's being kept. Is that enough for your igni?"

I raise my pointer finger and look around the room. "Does that work for you guys?"

Blessed silence is my only reply. I'll take that as a *yes*.

"The igni are good," I say. "What do you know about Lucifer's Gauntlets?"

"As I said, Luce trained us all for battle," answers Dad. "The gauntlets were a part of that. They were bracers, a kind of protection for your forearm. Lucifer's were made of gold and fashioned with a pattern of angel's wings. If you wore them, you could touch someone's chest and pull out their magical powers. The abilities would be stored in some kind of magical jars. I don't remember the name."

"Canopic jars?" offers Lucas.

"That's right. It was temporary, of course. Luce pulled out our powers during archangel battle practice. That forced us to fight as regular mortals and improved our skills as archangels. After battle training, Luce gave us our powers back." Dad leans back in his chair. "I saw the segment on *Good Morning Purgatory*. Based on what you've told me, the Viper must be using the gauntlets to steal other people's powers."

"That's right," I confirm. "Drayden is the key guard over Lucifer's prison. The Viper stole the power to make ghoul portals, snuck into the prison, and poisoned Drayden. That's the countdown. It's how long Drayden has left to live."

"Walker went to cure Drayden," adds Lincoln. "But something must have gone wrong. Myla and I suspect Inferno, the lava angel we met in Purgatory. The Viper used Lucifer's Gauntlets to raise her from the dead. However, when Inferno came back to life, her body was made of lava."

"Lava?" asks Dad. "That's impossible. I've never heard of magic like that."

"Anything is possible if you play around with spells enough," says Lucas. "And if you're willing to make a great enough sacrifice."

"True enough," replies my father. His eyes glaze over in thought. "I'll always remember the sacrifice of those seraphim." Dad shakes his head and refocuses on me. "What else did you learn?"

"Nothing good," I say. "Whatever the Viper is doing with Lucifer's Gauntlets, he thinks he can steal Lucifer's powers."

All the color drains from my father's face. "That is a terrible idea. This Viper has no chance against Lucifer—I don't care what sort of powers he's gained. Lucifer will kill him, get free, and start another holy war."

"Which is why we have to find Walker and cure Drayden." Pulling off my watch, I set it on the tabletop. "Let's cover this next. Walker said if he got in trouble rescuing Drayden, this watch would start a countdown *plus* display information needed for a rescue. I tried pushing buttons on the thing, but it hasn't shown any info. Only the countdown."

Dad starts to rise. "If you're talking about Lucifer's prison location, I should leave. Even after all these years, I don't trust myself knowing where Luce is kept."

Cissy turns over the watch in her hands and winces. "Don't worry. We won't get any information from this thing. This case is broken."

My heart sinks. "I was afraid of that."

Cissy hands the device over to Lucas. "What do you think?"

"I'll cast a small spell to see what we're dealing with." Lucas presses the watch between his palms and murmurs an incantation. A small poof of purple light and smoke emerges from between his hands. *Magic.* Excitement zings through my veins. Lucas is the best warlock in the House of Striga. Surely, he can get the watch to work.

Please, get the watch to work.

With the spell over, Lucas examines the watch once more. "I have bad news."

A fresh weight of worry settles onto my shoulders. "Let's have it."

"I'm afraid the physical damage nullified my spells," says Lucas. "That's my fault. I shouldn't have tied my magic to the watch's structure. We aren't familiar with technology here in Antrum."

And Lucas isn't lying, either. Thrax are totally stuck in the middle ages.

Cissy pops open her briefcase. "Don't worry, I brought

supplies. Lucas and I will start right away. If anyone can get data from this watch, it's us." She pulls out a new watch from the case, fiddles with the invisible buttons, and then hands it over to me. "This is the same watch, but without Walker's info. I just set it up so it always shows the countdown and time."

"Thanks." I slowly take the new watch from her hands. Walker's device needs to stay with Lucas and Cissy—that's our best chance to get the info we need—but I do hate parting with it.

"There was an image on that watch. It's the crest of the House of Victoriana. Walker was visiting them. Lincoln and I believe we need to track where those thrax go when they visit the Dark Lands. There may be some clues there." I'm careful not to say it's where Lucifer's prison is located. Dad looks jittery enough as it is.

Next I look to Lucas. "Long story short, Lincoln and I will need to do more sneaky things at Transfer Central. Do you mind doing cleaning up again after we're done?"

Lucas bows his head. "Whatever you require."

Cissy rummages around in her briefcase, pulls out a small flip-top cell phone, and hands it to me with a flourish that would make a game show hostess proud. "You can use this in the Dark Lands. It's loaded with everyone's phone numbers."

I examine the new device. "Wow, this is perfect." The last phone Cissy got me had tons of not-a-buttons that were called apps. I didn't know how to use the thing. But this device is super basic—ideal for a non-techie like me.

"I'd forgotten how the Dark Lands have cell service," says Lincoln.

"Let me get this straight," says Dad slowly. "I can call my daughter from the phone here on the wall ... and it will ring on that small device in the Dark Lands." My father has been around since the dawn of time. Even so, any technology outside of fast cars isn't his thing.

"Absolutely," says Cissy. "It's true that we don't have cell service in Purgatory, but they do have it in the Dark Lands. You can just use the wall phone and it will connect to Myla's cell."

"We don't have cell service *yet*," corrects Mom. "My people are working on it."

"A cell phone in the Dark Lands," I murmur. "That opens up possibilities." My mind spins through options.

Lincoln slips his arm around my shoulders. "What's your plan? I can see one cooking behind your eyes."

Mom brightens. "If you go to the Dark Lands, Xav and I will watch Maxon, of course."

I pause from my internal deliberations to eyeball Mom's suit. "Don't you have a big conference this week? I heard something about a mayor's convention. They're all worried about the Viper and safety stuff."

"Mayor's convention?" All the color drains from Dad's face. "I'm not sure I can handle Maxon alone."

"Don't worry," says Mom. "I can lead a little convention and my grandson at the same time." She gives Dad one of her dazzling smiles. "Plus, it will be fun."

My father slowly returns her grin with one of his own. "Yes, it will be." He shifts his focus to me. "What's your plan of attack? I can't wait to hear it."

I bob my brows. "I'm almost tempted to move to the briefing room."

"Like father, like daughter," he replies. I'd never thought about it before, but I probably did inherit my love of battle planning from him.

"Here's what I'm thinking," I begin. "Ciss and Lucas, you two work on the watch. See if you can extract Walker's rescue data. Mom and Dad take care of Maxon. Lincoln and I will visit wherever the Victoriana go in the Dark Lands. It's now..." I check my new watch. "1:47 pm. What do you say if Lincoln and I call the house phone here at say, 9 pm?"

"An excellent plan," states my father. His face beams with so much pride, I could burst.

All of a sudden, the vague thought I'd been trying to capture comes into clear focus. And it has to do with snooping.

"One last thing," I turn to Cissy. "Can you have your agents check out Enmity Farms? They were acting super strangely this morning."

"On it," says Ciss. "I've wanted an excuse to investigate those guys." Cissy is so excited, her golden retriever tail starts wagging.

"In that case, we're done here." I rise, which I've found is the fastest way to end a meeting. Otherwise, people can hang out and chat for ages.

We say our goodbyes and head off to our various tasks. All the while, my thoughts keep circling back to that countdown.

Less than a day remains to help Drayden. And how much time is left to save Walker, if any?

That's the real question.

*a*n hour later, Lincoln and I stand inside the closet Pulpitum of the Boudoir of Striga. Lincoln still wears his body armor; I've changed into my dragonscale fighting suit. Like my tail, this outfit is impervious to heat. No more burned-up clothing for yours truly. Like last time, Lincoln sets his hands at my waist; I loop my arms around his neck. My insides flutter with worry.

Time to head for the Dark Lands. Walker must be there.

Shaking my head, I try to focus on something other than Walker. A question appears. "Is Juliana still on duty at Transfer Central?"

"Absolutely," answers Lincoln.

"Do you think Lucas already…" I tap my temple, meaning: *did Lucas already wipe her memory?*

"One way to find out." Lincoln raises his voice. "I am Lincoln Vidar Osric Aquilus, activating Pulpitum transfer station."

A familiar voice fills the tiny space. "Your Highnesses. What a surprise. I'm your transfer agent, Juliana."

Lincoln and I share a long look. *Lucas stopped by already.*

Juliana, Lincoln, and I then go through the same routine as

our last Pulpitum ride. Juliana is all shocked that our station is marked as *unknown*. Lincoln and I repeat those all-out lies about Lucas stopping by to fix the problem. In short order, we're ready for the next step.

"Where would you like to go?" asks Juliana.

"That's a little complicated," explains Lincoln. "Can you scan the console for the last time someone from the House of Victoriana used the Pulpitum for transfer?"

"Yes, Your Highness." Some tapping noises sound. "It says Pulpitum VII." More tapping. "That's funny. It looks like the destination was written over. The text is flashing."

When I ask my next question, I'm careful to keep my voice low. "Who do you think did that?"

"My guess is Lady Snead," whispers my guy. "She's from House Victoriana and *currently* works in Transfer Central." The way Lincoln says the word *currently*, I suspect Lady Snead needs to shine up her resume.

"Is Pulpitum VII your destination?" asks Juliana.

"No, it's a different station," says Lincoln. "This is Lincoln Vidar Osric Aquilus, launching audible override. Show last destination."

"Oh, that did it," says Juliana brightly. "Now the console reads … this can't be right. *Unknown – the Dark Lands*. That's not an official transfer station."

My heart lightens. "It's where we want to go."

"Are you certain?" asks Juliana. "Maybe we should wait for Lucas."

"Myla and I will depart now for the Dark Lands," orders Lincoln. "Have you set the destination into the console?"

Additional clicking noises sound as Juliana does *whatever it is they do* in Transfer Central. Nervous energy zings through my limbs. How I hate waiting for the battle to start. Or the food to cook. Or anything, really.

"How's it going out there?" I ask.

"Ready," announces Juliana.

"Thank you," says Lincoln. "Initiating Pulpitum transfer in 3, 2, 1."

The platform lurches under our feet. Dark earth and mineral deposits speed past us as the round disc hurtles through the ground. Maybe it's just me, but the transfer seems to take way longer than usual. I start counting magma deposits as they speed by, just to keep myself from screaming. Finally, the Pulpitum platform comes to a jarring halt.

At this point, I know a few things for certain.

We're outside somewhere.

Our surroundings are thick with fog.

That's it.

A figure steps out of the mist: a young girl of about twelve. She wears an old fashioned, high-necked red dress with a bustle in back. Her ebony skin is flawless, and his dark hair is pinned back in a neat bun. She eyes me and Lincoln.

"You're not Walker," she says simply.

"No," I state. "We're friends of his."

The girl steps closer. Now I can see her mismatched eyes. *Thrax.*

"And you hail from House of Victoriana," states Lincoln.

"I'm Happy. Before you ask, that's my real name."

"Well, I'm Myla. This is Lincoln."

"Knew that already," replies Happy.

My tail waves to the girl over my shoulder. I pat the arrowhead end. "Agreed. I like her, too."

Happy goes on tiptoe to scan the mists behind us. "Is Walker with you? He was supposed to meet me here hours ago."

"We don't know where Walker is," says Lincoln. "We were hoping you knew."

"This is bad." Happy shakes her head. "Less than a day remains in the countdown."

"You know about that?" I ask.

"I know a lot of things," says Happy. She scans us carefully once more. "Question is, should I send you packing?"

"We're your king and queen," states Lincoln.

I raise my hand. "Also the Great Scala."

Happy shrugs. "That does nothing for you here." Her forehead crumples as she considers things. "Oh, well. There's nothing to be done about it. You know Walker. Perhaps you can be some kind of help. I'll lead you through the Whispers."

Say what? It's like this girl is talking in code. "The Whispers?"

"That's where you are," explains Happy. "This is a place that doesn't exist on a map that's long been forgotten. Victoriana built the Whispers and we keep its residents safe. I'll show you." Happy steps off into the mist, pauses, and then turns around. "Oh, if you see a molten lava angel? Stand back and let me handle it."

"You want to take on Inferno alone." My mouth falls open with shock. "But you're twelve and wearing a dress."

Happy folds her hands neatly at her waist. "I'm also the Chosen One of the Victoriana. Inferno should be afraid of me."

"Chosen One?" asks Lincoln.

Glad I'm not the only person who's lost here. I haven't been exposed to thrax culture for very long. For all I know, every house has a Chosen One who runs around other realms in period costume. Thrax can be weird that way. For instance, someone from every house has to dress up like a sheath of wheat once a year to celebrate harvest. Why celebrate harvest when you live underground? Like I said, weird.

"Well, now you know," says Happy. "Once a generation, someone like me is born to our house. And when I'm in the Dark Lands? I have powers you can't imagine." Her mismatched eyes glow, one red and one blue.

I must admit it. That's a cool trick right there. Plus, Lucas had mentioned that the Victoriana had some unique magic related to the Dark Lands. Things are looking up. With any luck, Happy's secret ability is tracking down lost ghouls.

"Stay close," orders Happy. "We're heading for Black Wing Manor." She marches off into the mist.

"You think she's legit?" I ask Lincoln.

"I do," he replies. "You don't get that kind of sass without serious power to back it up." My tail rises over my shoulder to lean toward Lincoln, the arrowhead end balled into a fist shape. Lincoln bumps my tail's makeshift 'fist' with his real one.

Those two.

I roll my eyes. My tail and Lincoln have their own mutual appreciation society. I suppose it's better than hating each other.

"Come along now!" calls Happy from the mist. "If you get lost, I am not running after your royalness."

"See what I mean?" asks Lincoln. "Serious power. Serious sass."

"I heard that!" calls Happy. "And you're damned right."

Lincoln and I share a smile. *She even swears like me.* I can't wait to see what this girl can do.

Maybe together, we'll save Walker and Drayden.

CHAPTER 13

*L*incoln and I follow Happy through the swirling mist. Although it's not just mist. It's some super heavy, *Jack The Ripper stalks you at night* style haze. Here and there, a bare tree branch becomes visible. That's all. Mostly, my mind imagines shapes in the haze. Or to be accurate, I only see one shape over and over: Walker screaming in pain. Not gonna lie. Thinking about Walker makes my blood pressure spike and fills my head with questions.

And what's happening to Walker right now?

Can we save Drayden in time?

Are they both howling in agony somewhere?

At last, the mist lessens. A massive, all-black mansion appears in the distance. If I thought my parents' place was serious Goth, their house has nothing on this monstrosity. I swear, even Dracula and Frankenstein would be like, *whoa that's over the top.* The thing is all turrets, big shutters, and little windows with arches over them. Also, the roof is super-pointy and topped with what look like metal curlicues. A tall and intricate iron fence encircles the grounds.

Seeing the house sparks a memory. I turn to Lincoln. "I saw

this place on Walker's watch. The iron gate is the same and everything."

"Good. Walker must have wanted us to come here."

Up ahead, Happy stops. The movement reminds me of what happens when a wild animal smells a predator on the air. Happy freezes mid-step, all her senses on alert.

Lincoln and I pause as well. My pulse slows. Inside my soul, my inner wrath demon awakens. She senses danger and relishes the chance for battle. Lincoln and I pull our baculum from their holsters. No point igniting them yet. The mist provides nice cover and angel fire would be a *kill me here* sign to any enemies.

Happy does that thing where she remains perfectly still but talks from one side of her mouth. "Listen to me carefully. Run past the gate. Once you're on the manor grounds, magic will protect you. She is near."

The scent of charcoal fills the air. No question who *she* is in this scenario.

Inferno.

"We're not leaving you," I say.

"Suit yourself." Happy rubs her palms together in a slow and purposeful rhythm. I've seen that move before with Lucas.

She's preparing to cast a spell.

My tail arches over my shoulder, ready to strike. I scan through everything I know about Inferno. This is not your typical angel. If anything, Inferno operates more like a Limus demon. Those guys are all stretchy goop and attitude. To kill them, you can't just stab them. Nope. Only way to off a Limus demon is to set it on fire and they're D-E-A-D. Inferno must have a weakness like that. But what is it?

A memory returns. When I broke out of the grain bin, my tail had been holding Inferno's sword. Something about that weapon changed, only I couldn't see what had happened. My instincts tell me that's the key to Inferno.

Transformation.

The scent of charcoal grows stronger. The air shifts around us. Small red lights dance far above our heads. Inferno is far away now, flying through the heavy clouds. That won't last long. Demonic energy pulses through my limbs, preparing me for battle.

A moment later, Inferno's great molten wings appear above us. Lines of light and fire shift along her feathers. Heat rolls off her lava body. Inferno lands a few yards away from Happy.

One good thing about this mist: Inferno still hasn't spotted me and Lincoln yet.

Inferno rounds on Happy. "Where is Walker?"

Happy keeps rubbing her palms. If a six-foot tall magma angel bothers her, the girl doesn't show it. *Impressive.* Her mismatched eyes glow, one red, one blue. "Come closer and I'll tell you."

Now, Happy may not be worried about Inferno, but that lava angel scares the crap out of me. I've seen fully-grown warriors die in battle due to overconfidence. No way am I taking chances with a twelve-year-old girl.

Lincoln's thinking the same thing. He ignites his baculum into a long sword. "Happy needs some back up."

"Agreed." I ignite my own baculum into a pair of short swords.

With our weapons ready, Lincoln and I step into the gap between Inferno and Happy.

"Leave this place," I command. "Now."

"Mother Scala." Inferno eyes me like I'm a three-headed alien that sprouted out of the ground. "Why haven't you abandoned Walker?"

I frown. "How are we having this conversation again? Walker is my friend." I'd roll my eyes but I can't take my focus off an opponent mid-battle. "What, do I have to get a tattoo on my forehead for you to believe me? I. Like. Walker."

Sheesh, what a ghoul hater.

Lincoln scans Inferno's face carefully. A new kind of light

shines in my guy's eyes. I know that look; it's the one Lincoln gets when we're playing chess and he's figured out how to take down my king in three moves or less.

"Why do you care what happens to Myla?" asks Lincoln slowly.

Huh. Good question.

"I don't," replies Inferno. "My commander desires her to understand that ghouls are evil."

Lincoln's gaze turns more intense. "And who is your commander?"

Emotions shift across Inferno's face. There's shock, worry, and finally, rage. "Lucifer," she answers at last.

Not sure I believe her. Inferno took way too long to answer. Plus, there are way too many evil players at work in the after-realms who could benefit from someone like Inferno flying around. Sure, the Viper is top of the list, but what about Armageddon? He's always scheming. Plus, I wouldn't even put it past the House of Victoriana to be playing both sides of this somehow.

There's no extra time to contemplate. Inferno leaps into the air, her wings beating in a steady rhythm as she speeds toward Happy. My throat tightens with worry.

Happy pulls her hands apart. Small lightning bolts crackle between her palms. Her mismatched eyes stay locked on Inferno. "Get over here already. Let me touch you and this will all be over with."

So, Happy's power is touch. *Battle mode* kicks in as I scan through this new intel. A ton of touch spells can help in battle. Which one can Happy wield? It may change our plan of attack.

Inferno hovers just above Happy. Grinning, Inferno grips the hilt of her sword, holding the weapon as one would a spear. With Inferno chucking stuff from the sky, that takes away Happy's touch advantage. *Yipes.*

"Now I shall touch *you*," snarls Inferno. "With my blade."

Those words pull the plug on Happy's sass. The girl's eyes widen. "Oh," she whispers. "Damn."

The battle just turned, and things aren't looking good for Happy.

I focus on Lincoln. "Assault Plan Delta?"

This is thrax field code. Assault Plan Delta means we'll both attack Inferno by turning our baculum into nets made of angel fire.

Lincoln extinguishes his baculum. "Add in a SuperMyla and it's perfect."

Here's what Lincoln's comment is all about. Purgatory only gets old black and white movies; Superman's one of them. After hours of repetitive viewing, I still don't have an answer to a simple question: how does Superman fly? In my case, my demonic energy helps me jump crazy high, but I soon hit earth again because REALITY. Superman has no means for defying gravity, let alone propulsion. So in all fairness, there should be no Superman but there should be SuperMyla. I must monologue on this topic a lot, because the other thrax on demon patrol ask me for a SuperMyla whenever I need to leap crazy-high.

But I digress. Back to the battle.

I shoot Lincoln my most winning smile. "SuperMyla it is."

Kneeling down, Lincoln laces his fingers together into a stirrup shape. I extinguish my baculum, holding a silver bar in each hand. Nearby, Inferno hovers relatively near the ground so she can throw her sword and skewer Happy.

Pulling demonic energy into my limbs, I step onto Lincoln's threaded fingers. As my guy stands, he helps propel me into the air. Combine that with my demonic strength and I end up a few yards above Inferno.

"Net!" I call.

"Net," echoes Lincoln.

A net of white angel fire weaves between the baculum in my hands. The same happens to Lincoln's baculum below. My guy snaps his wrists and his baculum net flicks up into the air. Then the top of his angel fire creation meets the bottom of mine.

Perfect.

Rolling forward into a somersault, I swoop through the air. My goal? To land on the opposite side of Inferno. We've now created a massive net made of blazing angel fire. As we saw with Lincoln before, Inferno's body can't withstand this stuff.

Let's see how she likes being shredded.

As my boots slam onto the ground, our joint angel fire net slices through Inferno, cutting her into hundreds of tiny pieces. The Inferno bits cascade to the earth, reminding me of tiny molten comets. The black grass sizzles with each impact.

"Retract," orders Lincoln. His net disappears. I order my net to do the same and then watch the many pieces of Inferno. Shredding someone is more than a little creepy, but if it gets rid of this big bad permanently? I'm calling it a win.

Happy moves to stand beside me. Her dainty hand grips my lower arm. "Do you think you killed her for good?"

"Give it a second," I say.

Sadly, the many parts of inferno turn gooey and ooze toward each other. "Hells bells," I groan. "No, she'll recover."

"Let's get out of here," announces Lincoln. "To the manor!"

As Inferno reforms, we all race toward the gate that encircles Black Wing Manor. The fence itself is twelve feet tall and solid iron. A large archway marks the entrance. It's getting late, so I can't make out much of the detail on the gate itself.

We all cross the threshold.

A reformed Inferno speeds behind us, not noticing the gate. As Inferno tries to cross under the iron archway, her body slams into an invisible barrier. Bits of magma spark into the air. Inferno's lava face tightens into a scowl.

"Did the invisible barrier stop the big bad Inferno?" asks Happy.

Couldn't have put it better myself.

"We are coming," Inferno declares. "All of us. The entire Brimstone Legion. We will break into the manor and set Lucifer free." Her gaze locks on me. "Prepare to disavow your allegiance to lower beings, Mother Scala."

With that, it's official. I now have a lava angel stalker. Not to mention confirmation that Lucifer is imprisoned here. Talk about bizarre.

"Disavow lower beings." Holding up my arm, I mime writing nothing into thin air. "Making a note of that."

Inferno growls, turns around, and flies off into the mist.

Happy straightens her cuffs. Looks like that's her default move when she needs to get her head together. "Let's enter the manor, shall we?"

"Ho, there," I say. "What was your hand spell about?" I rub my palms together as a demonstration.

Happy gives me a *duh* dace. "Uh, magic."

Lincoln steps in. "What Myla means is that the next time we go into battle, it's best if we know what we're dealing with."

I hitch my thumb toward my guy. "What he said."

Happy shifts her weight from foot to foot. "I can't say."

Lincoln's *expert chess player* face returns. "And why can't you share that particular information?"

"My powers. This mansion. All our secrets. It's up to the magistrate to give permission to talk. Come on, I'll introduce you to him." She takes a few steps away and then pauses. "You're not following?"

I shrug. "There's a whole lot of crazy in what you just said. I'm not stepping into a trap."

"What she said," adds Lincoln.

Happy hugs her elbows. "I honestly appreciate what you just did for me. If I could explain everything, I would. It's clear you two are worried about Walker. So am I. If we want to help our friend, then we have to see the magistrate. Will you please see the magistrate with me?"

Lincoln and I exchange a quick look. There really is only one answer to that question.

"Yes," says Lincoln.

As we step toward the main door, I glance down at my new watch.

Eighteen hours remain.

Whoever this magistrate is, I hope he has some answers.

CHAPTER 14

*L*incoln, Happy, and I step along a gravel path toward Black Wing Manor. After hiking up a short flight of slate steps, we reach a massive wooden door. The knocker is bronze and formed into a raven's head, complete with ruby eyes. Happy goes up on tiptoe and slams the metal down.

Thud!

A moment later, the door opens to reveal a young guy with mismatched eyes and white blonde hair. His features are uneven —small nose, big ears, that kind of thing—but it all works for him. Unlike most thrax, he wears modern stuff, namely skinny jeans and a loose sweater. He focuses on Happy. "There you are! I was so worried about you."

Two things about this guy. One, it's good that Happy has someone who cares about her. The whole *wandering in the mist* thing had me worried. Two, although Happy's name is, you know, Happy, she isn't exactly Smiley Girl. Meanwhile, this dude is someone who radiates positive energy. He's not traditionally handsome, but he's still definitely attractive.

The guy steps back to allow us all to enter. "Happy, where have you been?"

"Waiting for Walker." Happy hitches her thumb over her shoulder. "I picked up these two." She turns to me and Lincoln. "Guys, this is Jaime."

"Your Highnesses." Jaime gasps.

Lincoln and I step inside. Happy slams the door behind us. In the biggest non-surprise of the day, the manor's interior is as black and foreboding as the outside. Everything is dark wood and carved in a pattern of ravens.

Edgar Allen Poe, manor for one.

"I didn't know royalty was visiting." Jaime glares at Happy. "No one told me."

"That's a pattern with Victoriana," deadpans Lincoln.

If I know my husband—and I do—then he's already planning how to add Black Wing Manor and the Whispers into about a hundred maps and reviews. My guy is not a fan of undocumented stuff.

Happy holds up her hands in the universal sign for *it wasn't me.* "I didn't know they were on their way."

"So, now we have guests *and* a lava angel problem." Jaime shudders. "Tell me Inferno didn't find you."

"Oh, Inferno found me all right." Happy gestures toward me and Lincoln again. "And these two sliced her up into little Inferno nuggets."

At this point, my head turns a little fuzzy. It's been a big day and somehow, Lincoln and I ended up in a Gothic house with a few mystery thrax. Not to mention their so-called magistrate, whoever that is.

I clear my throat. "Hey, guys. What if we start off with some introductions?" I need a little grounding, and some standard social routines could be a good start.

Jaime straightens his stance. "Of course, Your Highness. I am Jaime Victenus Aeyre of the House of Victoriana, Keeper of the Chosen One."

Happy cups her hand by her mouth. "He's my manny."

"Manny?" I ask.

"Man plus nanny. Manny. My parents insisted I have one." Happy fluffs the lace by her neckline. "I can take care of myself just fine, though."

"Not true." Jaime lifts his chin. "I'm also here to teach you, young lady. Social skills are a particular sore point."

I can't believe what I'm hearing. "Social skills? No way. She's a lot like me. Don't change a thing."

Happy actually smiles. "Did you hear that? The queen says I shouldn't change. Nyah."

Lincoln shakes his head. "Wow. She even does the *nyah* thing."

"Right?" I ask. "No one says *nyah* except for me."

"What?" Happy shrugs. "Nyah nyah nyah NYAH nyah. It's totally a useful form of communication."

Here it is. Another beautiful moment where I can appreciate something—in this case, Happy's sarcasm—despite the fact that the world is falling apart. Mom would be proud.

A booming male voice echoes through the reception hall. "Who dares enter my mansion?"

Aaaaaaaand the moment is over.

Jaime pales. "Oh, no. The magistrate."

Guess 'social rituals grounding time' is over. Oh well.

I shoot Jaime a thumbs-up. "Let's meet him. Anything to get us closer to finding Drayden and Walker."

"I forgot about Walker." Jaime turns to Happy. "How did your meeting go?"

"It didn't." Happy kicks at the floor with her heeled boot. "Walker never showed."

Lincoln takes my hand in his. "All the more reason for us to meet this magistrate of yours. We need information in order to find Walker."

"Bring them to me!" booms the voice once again.

"You're right," says Jaime. "We better go. The magistrate is this way." The thrax picks up a candelabra from somewhere because, *of course this place has hand-held candelabras lying around.* With his spooky lighting device in hand, Jaime marches off down a nearby passage. Lincoln, Happy, and I follow Jaime through a series of gloomy corridors. There are a lot of shadows, cobwebs, and dark wood carved with raven heads.

Sheesh. And I thought my parents' place was a downer.

"What can you tell us about this magistrate?" asks Lincoln.

Happy mimes zipping her mouth shut and tossing away the key.

"So nothing," says Lincoln. There's no missing the smile in his voice, though. My guy does appreciate sass in all its forms.

I'm not worried. Jaime is the more blabby of the two anyway. "How about you, Jaime?" I ask. "What can you tell us about the magistrate?"

"His name is Obsidian Kildare." Jaime says the same *Obsidian Kildare* the same way I might say *freshly baked brownie.* "And his official title is Magistrate of the Whispers and Black Wing Manor."

"We better pick up the pace," warns Happy. "The magistrate's already asked for you twice. We don't want him to lose his temper."

"So true," says Jaime. "You don't want Obsidian—I mean, the magistrate—to become angry. The magistrate is far more powerful than Happy." Jaime pauses before a set of wooden doors. Like the rest of the house, these are also huge, black, and carved up with ravens.

Happy eyes the closed doors. "You better go in first, Jaime. He's always nicer when he sees you."

A slight blush colors Jaime's cheeks. "Do you really think so?"

Happy rolls her eyes. "I only tell you about a hundreds times a day."

Jaime hangs his head. "I'm not so sure."

I raise my hand. "Guys? This is really cute, but open the freaking door already."

"My bad," gushes Jaime. "Obsidian gets me distracted." Jaime pulls open the door and steps inside yet another darkened room. *Surprise, surprise.*

Lincoln shoots me a questioning look. *Should we go inside right now?*

I tilt my head, considering. On one hand, this Obsidian guy has a short temper (as well as a limited design sense, considering how he slaps black paint and birds everywhere.) If we stroll in before Jaime can work his magic, the magistrate may be grouchy. On the other hand, WALKER. DRAYDEN. We're on a time schedule to save them both.

My tail seems to agree, since the arrowhead-shaped end starts pointing to the room's interior.

I point toward the opened doorway. *Let's go in.*

Sure, it may be a risk, but it could also save Walker and Drayden.

CHAPTER 15

$\mathcal{L}$incoln and I step inside a massive drawing room. Vaulted wooden ceilings arch above us. A threadbare red carpet lines the floor. The rest of the space is filled with a variety of high-back chairs, benches, and small tables, all of which are carved into the likenesses of ravens. One wall is filled with a fireplace that's framed by even more ravens, only this time the likenesses are stacked up, totem-style. A long bench sits before the fireplace; it's where the only other figure in the room is seated.

Obsidian Kildare.

He's tall and lean, with skin so pale it almost seems to glow. I'd guess his age at somewhere around thirty. Obsidian wears black body armor, which seems an odd choice for sitting before a fireplace, but who am I to judge? His long dark hair is pulled back with a scrap of leather. Even from a distance, it's clear this guy has even features and sharp bone structure.

Honestly? I can see why Jaime's crushing on Obsidian, even if the magistrate does shout orders like a bully. He's got that *powerful but angsty warrior* thing going.

Lincoln, Happy and I hang out just inside the doorway. Jaime strides over to Obsidian's bench. "Good evening." Even though the whole place is gloomsville, Jaime manages to give a genuine smile.

Obsidian flicks his eyes a fraction, but it's enough for his gaze to meet Jaime's. A long pause follows where there's a lot of staring and no talking. Not gonna lie. It's starting to get awkward here. And let's not forget the time crunch to save Walker and Drayden.

At last, Obsidian breaks eye contact. "Greetings," says the magistrate. "Are you well, my friend?"

Jaime's blush deepens. "I'm fine."

"I detected strangers in my house."

Happy was right to suggest Jaime enter the room first. The bellowing magistrate from a few minutes ago is now Mister Nice Guy.

"The King and Queen of the Thrax are here," explains Jaime. "They're friends of Walker's."

That's our cue. Lincoln and I step deeper into the room. Obsidian watches our every move intensely. As we get nearer, I get a better view of the magistrate. He's one of those dudes with a young appearance and ancient eyes. In other words, there's magic at work here. Obsidian could be any old age, really.

Lincoln and I pause by the fireplace. My husband speaks first. "I am Lincoln Vidar Osric Aquilus, King of the Thrax and Consort to the Great Scala."

This isn't our first formal introduction. No question what my line is here. "I'm Myla Lewis, Great Scala and Queen of the Thrax."

"And why are you both here?" asks Obsidian. For the first time, I notice how Obsidian holds a tall wooden rod in his right hand. Firelight dances across the carving atop the staff: a raven's head with ruby eyes.

"It's like Jaime told you," I say. "We're friends of Walker."

Happy steps closer. "Walker never met me today."

At those words, Obsidian starts bellowing again. "What? How can that be? We're almost out of time!" He stomps his staff against the ground, one slam for every word he next speaks. "Where is Walker?"

"Hey, noisy." I mock-cover my ears. "We're looking for him too, all right? That's why we're here. By any chance, is the *time you're running out of* add up to …" I check my watch "… eighteen hours, twenty minutes and thirty-two seconds?"

Obsidian grips his staff so tightly, I'm surprised the wooden thing doesn't snap. "How do you know this?"

"As we said, Walker is our dear friend," says Lincoln smoothly. "He gave us valuable information so we could help his brother Drayden. Now we're searching for Walker as well. It seems we have some similar goals. Tell us what you know; we may be able to help you find Walker."

A low moan sounds through the air. It's a man's voice, deep and pained. Something about it cuts through my soul.

"Who made that noise?" asks Lincoln.

"Who indeed?" Obsidian shifts on his bench. "If you truly know Walker, then that question proves that he didn't trust you. I can't share our secrets with strangers and spies. Criminals have broken into Black Wing Manor. Liars. Thieves. Poisoners. I won't have it!"

Jaime steps closer to our side. "Queen Myla and King Lincoln aren't evil spies. These are my sovereigns."

Obsidian scowls. "They rule over you? All the more reason to suspect your judgment regarding their true nature."

"They're good people," adds Jaime. "Everyone likes them."

Now, this whole situation is pretty nasty, but I must admit one thing. It's nice to hear one of your subjects spontaneously say that you're good people.

Next Happy moves nearer to us. "Plus, Myla here is the daughter of the archangel Xavier. Lincoln's descended from the archangel Aquila. Why don't you cast a few spells? Check into their hearts? They're truthful, kind, and they care deeply for Walker. Let's be honest. Black Wing Manor has never faced so many problems before. Trespassers. Thieves. Poison. Inferno."

Obsidian doesn't reply. Instead he keeps glaring into the crackling fireplace. I open my mouth, ready to interject, but Happy steps in first.

"I'm here to protect and advise you," she says. "We need help. Trust these two. That's my advice."

My brows lift. *Happy is here to protect Obsidian?* My thoughts return to our last fight with Inferno. Happy was doing some kind of magic with her palms. Still need more specifics on what her powers might be. Something for later.

Seconds tick by before Obsidian stomps his staff onto the ground again. *SNAP!* This time the noise is so loud, it makes me shiver. Using the staff as leverage, Obsidian stands to his full height and turns to face us. It's a good thing this hall is huge, because something massive spreads out behind him.

Three set of wings.

Whoa.

I thought my father had a huge wingspan, but he only has one set. This guy almost fills the space. And all three sets are lined with black feathers.

"You're a seraphim," whispers Lincoln. "You have three sets of black wings."

Obsidian lifts his chin. "Yes."

I frown, trying to process this bit of news. The fact that Obsidian is a seraphim would explain a few things. Like why this place and its magistrate are not tracked on any map. Knowing they exist would burst the *'whole seraphim are dead'* bubble. Plus, the fascination with black-winged birds comes into clearer focus. As well as why Happy volunteered our angelic lineage. Even so, I can't get past what my father told me back in Purgatory.

"There's no easy way to say this," I wince. "But I heard the seraphim were dead."

"We are. I am." Obsidian shoots a glance at Jaime. Such pure longing shines in the seraphim's blue eyes, it breaks my heart. "I'm the last of my kind. Without my brothers and sisters, I might as well have perished."

The low moan sounds once more. The pained voice makes me jump. Lincoln's posture stiffens. Happy, Obsidian, and Jaime don't so much as flinch, though. Clearly, this isn't their first time hearing this particular misery. Yet another moan follows.

"Should we do something about that?" I ask. "Last I checked, moaning is not a good thing."

At this point, I can't ignore the possibility that the moaner in question is someone we know. My mind spins through ways to carefully raise the subject, but I'm not super at verbal fireworks. Best to just say it. "Have you imprisoned Walker or Drayden in here?"

"Did I imprison Walker or Drayden?" asks Obsidian.

Lincoln pulls his baculum from their holster. "That's what the queen asked."

Obsidian exhales a sigh that's just another way of saying: *fuck my life.* "No, I do not imprison anyone." The seraphim glares at Lincoln's baculum. "And do not attempt to face me in battle. You've no idea what I can do."

Not sure that's a great answer from Obsidian, but based on the tension in the room? I think we all need a breather.

Resting my hand on Lincoln's arm, I guide him to reset his baculum. "Look," I say. "My husband and I get that you need to check us out. So, why don't you cast those spells like Happy suggested? Then we can talk some more."

Emotions flicker across Obsidian's handsome face. Fear. Rage. Grief. His three sets of wings extend further out, then retract behind his back. "That is a wise course."

Happy rolls her eyes. The girl doesn't say '*duh*' but I can picture the word hanging in a thought bubble above her head.

"Indeed, I shall cast some spells," continues Obsidian. "In the meantime, the King and Queen may wait nearby. If all looks acceptable, I'll call you back here and share our *little secret*." The way Obsidian says *little secret*, I can tell it's a huge deal.

"Excellent choice, magistrate." Jaime brightens the room with another dazzling smile directed right at Obsidian. The seraphim meets the gaze for a fraction before looking away.

Obsidian then glares at me and Lincoln. "Know this. If I deem you unworthy, you'll never leave this manor again."

All of a sudden, a break sounds like a fabulous idea for me, too. I've officially had it with Obsidian for now. The dude is a lot of drama.

"Thanks for the clarity, Obsidian." I turn to Jaime. "Let's get to the *leaving this chamber* part of the evening."

"Of course," replies Jaime. "I'll take you to a waiting room."

"Bring them back to me in an hour," orders Obsidian.

Jaime bows slightly at the waist. "Yes, magistrate."

I get that Obsidian is a big bad seraphim, but the attitude is a little over the top. My tail seems to agree. As we leave, my tail shoots Obsidian a modified version of a lewd hand gesture behind my back. It's somewhat satisfying, but not as good as mouthing off directly.

Too bad I need Obsidian in order to save Walker and Drayden. Otherwise, I'd sass off to him and how.

CHAPTER 16

$\mathcal{O}$nce we leave Obsidian, Jaime leads us on a long walk through more dark passageways. We hike a few wide, winding staircases. What Black Wing Manor lacks in terms of design diversity, it certainly makes up for in space. In other words, this place is a big-ass mansion decorated with a shit-ton of ravens.

Jaime leads us to a sparse room. A few simple wooden chairs line the walls. There's one window—that's too small to sneak out of—and which is covered in black glass. And yes, everything in here is made from dark wood. At least there are no raven carvings. *Bonus.*

Jaime makes his goodbyes and shuts the door. The moment Lincoln and I are alone, something vibrates against my chest. I gasp. Did someone hit me with a spell? Then I remember it.

My phone from Cissy.

My dragonscale fighting suit doesn't have pockets (total design flaw but I love the outfit anyway.) Cissy gave me this clippy necklace to hold my new phone under the suit. Now that device is shimmying against my rib cage. Pulling out the phone, I flip it open and see XAV AND CAM written on the little screen. I push the very-easy-to-understand *call* button.

"Myla? Are you there?" My father sounds pretty freaked. Although, based on how confused he was about calling a cell phone from a wall phone, this might just be technology angst I'm dealing with here.

Lincoln narrows his eyes. "Who is it?"

"My father," I reply to Lincoln. Then I speak to the phone. "What's going on, Dad? It's only seven o'clock. We're not supposed to talk until nine." My pulse speeds. "Did you learn something about Lucifer's Gauntlets or Inferno?"

"It's terrible," says Dad. "Your mother got called off for that mayor's meeting. She isn't here and Maxon got..." He inhales a long breath.

Hells bells. Something is wrong with my baby. My body feels like I instantly plunged into an ice bath. Lincoln has dad-sense, so he pauses too. His mismatched eyes lock with mine. Every line of my guy's face is etched with worry.

I force in a deep breath. "Just tell me what happened."

"Maxon has ... a diaper rash."

I wait for the rest of the story. It can't be *Maxon has a diaper rash* and that's it. "Oooookay. Diaper rash. And what else?"

"Didn't you hear me?" Dad's voice takes on a note of hysteria. "His bum is all red."

"So that's diaper rash." I make a conscious effort to sound super calm. "Got it."

Beside me, Lincoln relaxes. The words 'diaper rash' did the trick. Lincoln launches into one of his classic activities when entering a new space: inspecting the walls to find hidden doors and such. Antrum is filled with these secret passages, and my guy can uncover them like you wouldn't believe.

"Yes, it's diaper rash," Dad continues. "So I found the diaper cream and put it on. Here's my question. How much is too much?"

My forehead crumples with confusion. *What exactly happened here?* "Tell me what you did."

"Well, you know how butts have a crack?"

How am I having this conversation with my father? "Yes."

"Well, I can't see his little butt crack anymore. Only the rash cream. Is that too much?"

I have to bite my thumbnail to stop from laughing. "Yes, that's definitely in the realm of *too much.*"

"Oh, no." Footsteps sound. Dad's pacing his office. "That cream is medicine. Do you think I've poisoned him?"

"No, get a towel or something and wipe off the extra cream. You just need a light amount."

"But I thought that *was* a light amount. I only used one tube."

"No, Dad. One tube of diaper cream is too much diaper cream." I'm biting my lips together now, the urge to laugh is so hard. "Put on the stuff like you would sunscreen."

"Sun … screen?" Dad says the word like I just spoke gibberish.

"Oh, that's right. You don't get sunburn. Forget that example. Put it on like you're buttering bread."

"Still not following."

"I forgot again. You don't eat food, either." The last year or so, my father has been experimenting with meals in order to seem more human. The results have been a little nasty, especially when he tried cooking fish without removing the scales. Took us a month to air out the kitchen.

I pinch the bridge of my nose. *What kind of example can I use?* My eyes widen. I snap my fingers. "I've got it. It's like when you're fighting an Ocular demon, and you need to apply ionic balm to its tail and bind it."

"Ooooooh." Cool relief sounds in my father's voice. "I got it now. Better run."

"Wait," I say. "Any updates for us?"

"Updates?" My father sounds genuinely confused.

"Any news about Walker and Drayden? Or the wristwatch

Ciss and Lucas are working on?" I'd wonder how my father forgot our entire mission, but my son has a way of commanding attention.

"Oh, that! Well, I'll be honest. I've been too worried about this diaper rash for anything else. Mortals are incredibly fragile. Maxon could have died!"

"Maxon would not have died from diaper rash."

All this time, Lincoln has been checking the floorboards. At my latest words to Dad, Lincoln looks up and grins. I know what my guy is thinking. *Your father is a character.*

I roll my eyes. *I know.*

"Oh, wait!" cries Dad. "There's an envelope on my desk. It's Cissy's writing." Tearing sounds echo as my father opens the letter.

For the record, I am so thankful Cissy accepts my father's technological limitations and sends off messengers with written missives.

"It says here that Cissy and Lucas had no luck in fixing the watch. Lucas is taking the device to Antrum to see if anyone in Striga can help." In case you're wondering, my father's the type who never reads exactly what someone wrote down; he always summarizes. It's a habit from sharing battle updates.

"Also," continues Dad. "Cissy and Zeke left for the Enmity brothers farm. That's it."

A series of knocks sound at the door, breaking up my thoughts. Crossing the small room, Lincoln pulls the door open.

Jaime stands in the outer hallway. He raises his candelabra. "Obsidian is ready."

Lincoln narrows his eyes. "It hasn't been an hour."

Jaime shrugs. "His spells finished faster than anticipated." He lowers his voice. "You checked out rather quickly."

"Good to know," says Lincoln.

I refocus on my chat with Dad. "Have to run. Call me if you find out anything more."

We say our byes and I hang up the phone. With Jaime's guidance, Lincoln and I leave the so-called waiting room and start another long trek through Black Wing Manor. Only this time, we keep descending one spiral staircase after the next. All signs of raven carvings disappear. The walls become nothing but rough stone. Cobwebs drip from the ceiling. The air turns stale.

At one point, I might not have known what all this means. But now, I jointly rule Antrum, and that realm is located deep underground.

Wherever we're going, it's down.

CHAPTER 17

$\mathcal{A}$s Lincoln and I descend the stairs for our mystery meeting with Obsidian, the moaning sounds return. Only now, they're much louder. My heart pounds so hard, my pulse beats in my temples.

Who is hurting?

Are Lincoln and I next?

My thoughts race through battle and escape options. Lincoln is an expert tracker. No matter what bizarre route Jaime took to our destination, my guy will find a way out. Nope, the bigger question is this: *what will we discover with Obsidian?* I had enough trouble fighting a lava angel for the first time. Seraphim are master mages. Beyond that, I know zero about how they might act in battle.

At last, we reach a stout wooden door. It's set into the stone wall and has a metal slider-handle. Basically, this is your classic dungeon set up. I check my baculum. *Yup, they're still in a holster at the base of my spine.* Lincoln has his as well. If Obsidian wants to imprison us here—or worse—then we'll put up a fight.

Jaime pauses by the door. For a guy who's normally pretty smiley, his face droops into the mother of all frowns. "Your Highnesses," Jaime intones. "No matter what you see or learn here, you must respect Walker's wishes. Do I have your solemn vow?"

My thoughts return to the Enmity Farms trip with Walker one day and two million years ago. "I gave Walker my word that I'd help him and Drayden. Whatever you're about to show us—is it all part of Walker's plan?"

"It is," says Jaime solemnly.

"Then you have my vow," I say.

"And mine as well," adds Lincoln.

Jaime pulls on the slider handle. The door unlocks with a heavy thud. Pressing his shoulder against the wood, Jaime forces the door to swing open. The scent of sweat and mold wafts into the outer hallway.

Lincoln and I step closer to the threshold.

At first, all I see is Obsidian. He stands at the far wall of a large stone room. *That's good.* If this were some kind of trap, Obsidian probably wouldn't wait inside. I shift my gaze to Lincoln. My guy gives me the barest of nods. I know he's thinking the same thing as I am.

Let's go in.

With hesitant steps, I slip inside the stone room. I'm completely unprepared for what I discover.

The chamber is large, square in shape, and completely made of gray rock. A low, flat boulder sits in the center of the space. Atop that rock crouches a man with pale skin who is stripped down to his waist. His back faces us; it's easy to make out the column of his spine.

I lace Lincoln's hand with mine. Together we step closer.

Suddenly, the man's skin changes. Images appear on his flesh: a pattern of intricate lines. Zings of recognition move down my back. This design is familiar; I saw it in Walker's phone. It's an aerial view of a labyrinth that's drawn with the precision of an architect. Every few seconds, the image changes. Walls move. Doors close. The maze adapts. But why?

"Come in," says Obsidian. I scan his face carefully, looking for any sign of an ambush or other tricks. His features are unreadable.

I grip Lincoln's hand more tightly, pulling strength from our connection. *Together, we can do anything.* With careful steps, we walk around the low boulder. As we move closer, the man seated atop the stone doesn't so much as glance our way. At last his face comes into view.

He's a ghoul who looks just like Walker.

Only he isn't Walker.

"Drayden?" I ask, my voice shaking. "Is that you?"

The ghoul doesn't seem to hear me.

Like Walker, this ghoul has a whip-strong build and high cheekbones. Beads of sweat dot his bald head. His eyes are large, all-black, and stare forward as if in a daze.

Lincoln takes up the question. "Drayden?"

"He's changing the maze," says Obsidian. "He won't respond to anyone for hours."

I look over my shoulder, hoping to find Jaime. But the manny has left. Not that I blame him. This is one bizarre situation, right here.

"His skin." I swallow past the knot of anxiety in my throat. "It's covered with a labyrinth map."

"Yes." Obsidian taps the ground with his staff. "That's the maze right below our feet. It's where we imprison Lucifer. Drayden must change it regularly in order to keep Lucifer contained. That archangel is rather clever."

Drayden lets out another low moan.

Anger heats my blood. "You said you didn't imprison him."

"This isn't a prison," retorts Obsidian. "Drayden chose to become Labyrinth Master. He considers it an honor to keep the after-realms safe from Lucifer."

That sounds like Drayden, all right.

I scan Drayden more carefully. All ghouls are already pale, but

Drayden's skin has also taken on a greenish hue. "Walker said he was poisoned."

Sadness glistens in Obsidian's blue eyes. "Yes, the Viper snuck into the manor and shot a poison directly into Drayden's veins. Drayden couldn't escape from the villain. And as Labyrinth Master, he can't even be healed. Drayden must remain magically merged into the labyrinth itself."

For the first time, I focus closely on Drayden's frame. While couching atop the stone, Drayden balances on his hands and feet. When I see it, a gasp escapes my lips. Drayden's hands are magically combined with the stone. Rock covers those limbs up to his wrists.

No wonder Walker is so desperate to free his brother.

"How long has Drayden been here?" asks Lincoln.

"2,132 years," replies Obsidian. "Drayden has been our longest standing Labyrinth Master. Then again, his angelic gift of intellect has aided him immensely. I believe he could have lasted forever, if not for the poison."

"Two millennia," I whisper.

"Now you know our secret," intones Obsidian. "We wait here and protect Lucifer's prison. The gate and fence magically guard the manor. The Chosen One has additional power to help keep our enemies at bay. Recently, that Viper criminal found his way in here. Believe me, once I find the Viper—and I *will* catch that fiend—then I dispose of the villain painfully." Obsidian steps closer to Drayden. "The Viper suffer for what was done to you."

Now, I'm ninety-nine percent sure I know the answer to this question, but I have to ask it anyway. I steel my shoulders. "And who is your next Labyrinth Master?"

"Why Walker, of course," says Obsidian.

I grip Lincoln's hand with such force, I'm surprised I don't break a bone. My thoughts race. So do my words.

"Let me get straight," I begin. "Walker and I were just at this worm farm. We discussed how Walker was going to this *disap-*

pearing place. I hoped he meant a beach. But he didn't. Walker is coming down here where his hands will be merged into a stone until what? He dies from exhaustion?"

"I'm not a monster," says Obsidian. "Before any Labyrinth Master agrees to the role, they know it's to the death. I made an exception for Walker and Drayden. If Walker takes over before the countdown ends, then I will save Drayden. But only if Walker becomes Labyrinth Master in time."

"Suppose Walker doesn't take Drayden's place?" asks Lincoln. "Is there another ghoul who can step in?"

"Now we come to my great folly," intones Obsidian. "Time was, I spent years cultivating possible Labyrinth Masters. I found clever ghouls who were willing to do anything in exchange for the right wealth or spell. But Drayden has been Labyrinth Master so long, I became complacent. Lazy. Foolish. I reached out to no ghouls and created no contingency plans. Now there are no other Labyrinth Masters ready to step in, only Walker. And if we don't find Walker? Inferno will get what she wants. Lucifer will be released in a matter of hours and ... you know what Lucifer will create."

A bloodbath.

My eyes widen. "I've got it. I'll summon my father. Only an archangel can destroy another archangel, right? He can get his buddies to together and do it."

"Hear my truth." As he speaks, Obsidian's eyes glow angel blue, so I know he means every word. "Your father and the other archangels tried to kill Lucifer many times before we seraphim stepped in. The challenges did not work. Your father and his peers lost every duel. They can not destroy Lucifer."

How I hate to admit this. "You're right. My father said ... something about that."

"We have only one solution here," states Obsidian. "We must find Walker and make him Labyrinth Master." Obsidian slams his staff onto the floor in a movement that says *conversation closed.*

"Which brings me back to why I've taken you into my confidence. You promised to help find Walker. To do that, you need more information. Happy will now give you show you our grounds. The manor includes several critical insights into Inferno which must be seen to be understood. After that, we'll see if you can be useful to the Whispers."

Okay, that was a lot of information. Not to mention the fact that while all that content went down, Drayden was moaning and making mazes nearby. It's all I can do to whisper two words. "Hells bells."

Obsidian stomps toward the door, then pauses by the threshold. "Know this. If you try to cross me, my magic will strike you down." The raven eyes on Obsidian's staff glow red. With that, Obsidian stalks out the exit.

For a long moment, it's just me, Lincoln, and Drayden. Eyes that look so much like Walker's still stare out into space.

Two millennia.

My feet seem to move on their own. With careful steps, I approach Drayden and kneel beside him. Every cell in my body feels charged with a mixture of fear and pity. Trembling, I reach forward and wrap my hand around Drayden's wrist. His skin feels cool and loose.

Poor Drayden.

"I don't know if you can hear me," I say in a low voice. "But I'm Walker's adopted sister. That makes you my brother, too." My eyes sting. I recall the image of Drayden's statue. How he stood tall in his angelic robes, a heavy book under his arm. Now Drayden is only skin, bones, and shifting labyrinth lines.

"You've sacrificed so much to help keep the after-realms safe," I say, my voice cracking. "Now, it's our turn to aid you."

Lincoln kneels beside me. Reaching forward, my guy wraps his hand around Drayden's free wrist. "Walker is my best friend. Myla is my wife. We'll fight for you with everything we have inside us."

The next words come tumbling from my mouth without any close screening from my brain. "And I swear to you, we *will* find a way to free both you and Walker. I'm not slapping my honorary older brother onto a rock until he's dead."

Drayden blinks and for the first time, his gaze focuses. He looks directly into my eyes. When he speaks, his voice is a hoarse croak. "Save ... Walker."

My heart just cracked in two, right there.

"We will," states Lincoln. "We swear it."

"How?" asks Drayden.

"Honestly?" I sigh. "We don't know yet." I'm tempted to add that we never know how we'll get out of these life-or-death situations. Not sure that'll be comforting.

Drayden gives us the barest of nods. After that, the blank look returns to his eyes. The labyrinth markings on his body shift faster.

Lincoln gently rests his hand at the base of my spine. "We should go." With soft movements, he guides me toward the door.

So glad one of us is functioning right now. Otherwise, I'm pretty sure I'd just kneel here and hang with Drayden.

Out in the hallway, Jaime waits for us. "I'll take you upstairs. Happy is waiting for us by the front door."

My head is officially foggy. I might say thank you, I'm not sure. I do know that Lincoln keeps his hand gently pressed against my back while we return to the manor house proper. With every step, my thoughts whirl through everything we just learned.

The Labyrinth Master.

Drayden's two thousand years.

Walker's horrible promise.

Lucifer's imminent release.

Back at the Enmity brothers' farm, I thought Walker was going into hiding temporarily. Or at least, he was going somewhere I could visit and-or convince him to escape from. But this?

I already vowed to save Drayden. Freeing Walker's brother isn't possible if it sets Lucifer loose. And I certainly can't allow Walker to become the next Labyrinth Master. There has to be another way.

Sadly, we have less than eighteen hours to find it.

Not looking good.

CHAPTER 18

I'm not too attentive about what happens next. Stairs are involved. Cobwebs. Raven carvings. At some point, there's a front door and a few hellos with Happy. Soon, Jaime, Happy, Lincoln, and I are marching down the front steps of Black Wing Manor. Not sure if it's day or night here. My guess is that it all looks the same. Heavy mist still covers the ground. I return to obsessively checking my watch. The latest countdown?

Seventeen hours, eighteen minutes, fifty-two seconds.

My stomach sinks to my toes. How can we save Walker and Drayden in less than a day?

Without meaning to, I let out an extra loud sigh. Lincoln takes my hand; his gaze locks with mine. "We will do this."

I give his palm a gentle squeeze. "Yes."

All the while, the four of us step along a gravel path that leads off the grounds. Beyond saying hello, there hasn't been much chatter. I stop before the gate's archway. Lincoln waits beside me.

My guy gives my hand a squeeze. "Is something wrong?" he asks.

"Not wrong," I reply. "I was just thinking. Once we cross under this archway, we're no longer protected by the magic of the fence that surrounds Black Wing Manor. Only, I don't see any sign of magic. Normally, there are ward stones or some sign of a spell."

Lincoln scans the nearby ground. "There's too much mist to be sure."

Happy's voice carries through the haze. "I'll show you where the magic comes from. Just follow me."

I shoot Lincoln a sly smile. "I guess my voice carries."

He winks. "It does."

Still hand in hand, we step under the archway and beyond the gates protection. Our small group makes a sharp left into the mist. We only walk a few yards when Happy pauses.

"We can stop right here," says Happy. "I'll clean things so you can get a better view."

I purse my lips. *Could Happy's magic involve controlling the weather?*

Happy turns to Jaime. "When was the last time we didn't have this fog?"

Jaime bobs his head, thinking. "About a month ago."

"Perfect." Happy rubs her hands together, just as she did when we first faced Inferno. Small bolts of lightning crackle between her palms. Happy then kneels and places her hands against the dark grass. When she speaks, her voice is deeper and rich with power. "I cast my spell. Return this place to one month ago."

White light bursts from Happy's palms, landing directly into the earth. The brightness flares across the landscape in concentric circles, reminding me of a stone being dropped in a pond. Only instead of a stone, it's Happy's magic. And what would be the pond is the landscape around Black Wing Manor.

The light flares more brightly before disappearing. The spell is cast. All around us, the mist instantly evaporates. A rolling green now appears before us, although the grass is more black than emerald. The sky stays dark with clouds, but at least the ground is visible. A sense of awe tingles through my limbs.

Before us, there stretches the largest graveyard I have ever seen. There are statues galore, all of them stacked up so closely, I wonder how many people died to warrant such a display.

"The way my power works is to—" Happy stops mid-sentence. Like before, she pauses with that alertness that only comes when sensing a predator. Happy slowly stands. As Happy's hands leave the Earth, her spell breaks. The mist slowly reappears, covering all the landscape in a milky haze.

That when I notice it.

An odd smell wafts on the air. I take in a deep breath and try to place the scent. Peat moss. Wet grass. Dust. Charcoal.

I give Lincoln's hand a gentle squeeze. "Is that?" I don't need to add the name *Inferno.*

Lincoln inhales as well. "I'm not sure."

Jaime rounds on Happy. "Whatever it is, we're going back to the manor. Now."

"It might not be her," counters Happy. "We must help both Drayden and Walker. Lincoln and Myla have to see *everything.*"

Jaime grabs Happy's hand. "I promised your parents I would care for you. That means we don't wait around for trouble."

The charcoal scent grows more intense. Dots of red light flicker through the mists above our heads. No question about it.

Inferno is coming.

"Everyone back to the mansion," I call. "Now!"

The four of us spin about and race toward the archway and the protection of manor grounds. Before us, Inferno appears out of the mist. Her great molten wings spread to full width, blocking the gate's entrance archway.

I set my feet shoulder width apart. My tail arches high. *Battle stance.*

"Plan Omega," says Lincoln.

This is a defense versus assault plan. Lincoln wants us to distract Inferno so Happy and Jaime can get away. *Great idea.* As an extra bonus, Plan Omega includes more of the acrobatic moves I love. Lincoln pulls out his baculum, igniting them into a spear.

"Agreed."

Now, my dragonscale fighting suit doesn't magically change like my Scala robes. That said, this outfit does have a few bonus features. I pull on the built-in gloves and yank the flame-resistant hood over my head.

There. Now I'm perfectly protected from fire.

Igniting my baculum into a pair of short swords, I race straight into a frontal assault. Inferno stands before the archway to enter the manor grounds. I speed toward her, leap into the air, and slam my boots onto her chest. My kick sends Inferno hurtling backward.

Right into the invisible barrier.

Like before, Inferno's back slams into the unseen wall that protects the manor. Sparks from her molten body shoot into the air. I land slap in front of her and jam my short swords through her chest and into the unseen wall behind her.

Inferno doesn't cry out with pain. Cutting this lava angel doesn't seem to hurt her in the slightest. But this time, she doesn't laugh. Why? I've stuck her to the invisible wall like a pin through a bug. Her molten boots even dangle a few inches above the ground.

Nyah.

Lincoln steps forward, his long sword held high. No question what he'll do next. Once Inferno is in little lava angel pieces again, Happy and Jaime can race onto the safety of the manor ground.

Lincoln stalks closer to Inferno. As he gets nearer, the lava angel grins.

Not a good sign.

"Watch out behind you," warns Inferno in a sing-song voice.

Normally, I wouldn't listen to advice from an insane molten

lava angel, but Inferno's claim has one thing going for it. Inferno is in front of me.

Intense heat slams into me from behind.

Damn.

I glance over my shoulder. Two more lava angels step out of the mist.

"Lincoln?"

My guy follows my gaze. "I see them."

Happy steps out of the mist. "You guys take on the other angels. I'll get Inferno."

Which brings me to another situation where norms don't apply. If this were any other day, I'd tell Happy to forget it. This is Inferno. Happy is twelve. But there are two molten lava angels running at me and Lincoln. Jaime is no warrior. At this point, I can only hope that Happy knows what she's doing.

Both of the new angels attack with long swords. Unfortunately, my baculum are still stuck in various parts of Inferno's rib cage. Before I can tell her to stop, Happy pulls my baculum out of Inferno, slicing the lava angel into three neat parts in the process.

Inferno is down. That won't last, though.

Turning to me, Happy tosses both baculum rods my way. "Here you go," she calls.

I catch them. "Be careful, Happy."

At that moment, a lava sword swipes an inch away from my nose. That would be the angels I've decided to call Charro 1 and Charro 2.

No time for further chatter with Happy. Igniting my baculum into a long sword, I meet Charro 1's thrusts, slice for slice. Beside me, Lincoln does the same with Charro 2.

Meanwhile, Happy rubs her hands together. Lightning sparks between her palms. The three pieces of Inferno ooze back together into one molten angel. The moment the process is complete, Happy places her palms against Inferno's stomach.

"I cast my spell," says Happy. "Return this angel to twelve years old."

A burst of white light flares out from Happy's palms. Once again, the effect reminds me of ripples on a pond. The last time she cast, Happy's spell changed a misty landscape into a vast graveyard. Now, her magic transforms the lava version of Inferno into a girl of twelve years old. No molten skin. No weapons. It's Inferno, only she's younger.

I'm so shocked, I almost get skewered by Charro 1.

"Pay attention," calls Happy. I'm not sure if she means that I should stay focused on my battle or on her, but there's no missing what Happy does next. Inferno stares forward with stunned blue eyes.

And Happy punches the young Inferno at that perfect spot on the jawline. WHAM! It's the point that cracks your bones and knocks you flat out. Young Inferno falls over like a sack of potatoes.

Jaime rushes up behind Happy, grabs her hand, and leads them both under the archway and into the safety of the manor grounds.

"Get over here!" cries Jaime. "Inferno won't stay down for long!"

Jaime doesn't need to tell us twice. We're so getting out of here. Too bad running means getting backstabbed by the Charros.

"SuperMyla!" calls Lincoln. He breaks his long sword into two short blades and takes on both lava angels.

And I know exactly what to do next.

Crouching down, I pull all my demonic strength into my legs. Pushing up, I leap high into the air, far above the heads of the two lava angels. As I descend, I split my own baculum into short swords and point the blade end downward.

As I land, I skewer the enemy molten baddies through the top of their heads. They scream. Loudly. Guess these guys are a little more sensitive than Inferno. Or maybe the top of the head is a touchie spot. Whatever the reason, the Charros fall over lifeless. Sadly, they won't stay that way for long.

Lincoln and I race back toward the manor, crossing under the archway just as Inferno retakes her molten form.

Let the record show that Inferno is not pleased. And for some reason, the only person she wants to yell at is yours truly. "I told you to abandon Walker and lesser beings. Why are you here?"

I pinch the bridge of my nose. "We are not having this conversation again. Buh-bye." Turning about, I back into the manor house. I'm about halfway to the door when I hear it. A male voice echoes through the mist.

"Happy! Myla! Lincoln!"

The tone is tortured, half dead, and utterly familiar.

Unholy Hell.

That's Walker.

$\mathcal{O}$nce more, Walker's voice echoes through the mist. "Myla! Lincoln! Happy!"

The three lava angels pause, share a few excited glances, and then take to the skies. There's no question what they plan to do.

Kill Walker.

My mind empties. Walker is here. We must help him. Trouble is, the mist is heavy and there are three lava angels in our way. Bands of terror tighten around my chest. All of a sudden, I can't pull in enough breath.

Lincoln calls through the mist. "We're coming for you, Walker!" After that, my guy turns to me. Trust and love shine in his mismatched eyes. When he speaks again, his voice is low and calm.

"Tell me when you have it."

Six little words, but there's a world of confidence behind them. Lincoln's saying that he trusts me to design a plan to save Walker. *We can do anything.* My breathing slows. Inside my soul, my inner wrath demon awakens. My thoughts whirl as my mind switches into *battle mode.* I run through the situation. Walker is nearby. Hurt. Frightened. And about to face down three lava angels.

An idea appears.

I turn to Lincoln. "I have it."

My guy grins. "I knew it."

With that set, I round on Happy. "When was the last time it rained?"

"I don't know." Happy gapes at me like I've lost it. "We must save Walker! He's out there alone with those lava angels." She starts to race for the gateway.

Jaime sets his hand on Happy's shoulder, stopping her. "Don't worry, I see what the Queen is doing." Jaime focuses on me. "There was a rainstorm here five days ago. A big one."

"Got it." Lincoln kneels down before Happy. He fixes her with the same confident look that helped to ground my soul. "When Myla and I give our signal, you work your magic. Take us back to five days ago. All right?"

Happy nods so quickly, I worry that she'll get whiplash. "Okay. Just get Walker."

With Happy set, Lincoln and I race past the gate and into the grounds beyond. We don't dare light up our baculum. The fog is so thick, it will hide us easily. The lava angels can't conceal themselves, though. Every so often, I see a flicker of their molten red in the distance.

As we step along, Lincoln scans the ground with an expert eye. Years of demon patrol on the Earth's surface means that my guy can find his way anywhere. We march along for a while before Lincoln sets his hand on my shoulder. The meaning of his motion is clear. *Time to stop.* Lincoln scans the mist carefully.

"Tough call," whispers Lincoln. "Attack plan Beta Nu or another Omega."

"Omega," I say in a low voice. "We shouldn't attack unless we're forced. Let's just get in, get out, and rescue Walker."

Tilting his head, Lincoln stares off into the mist even more intently. I have no idea what he sees, only that he's witnessing something. "Omega it is. Let's go. Can you give Happy the signal?"

"Will do." Inhaling deeply, I pull in demonic energy into my diaphragm and vocal cords. Then I let out an ear-splitting yell.

"HAPPY! NOW!"

White light bursts from behind us as Happy casts her spell. Once the light disappears, sheets of rain pour from the sky, clearing out the fog and revealing the landscape clearly.

Just before us lies Walker on the ground, his body curled up on his side. He's clutching something against his chest. Even from this distance, it's clear that his skin is marred with cuts and bruises. His ghoul robes are torn to rags. A combination of rage and sorrow heat my blood.

Inferno. The Viper. They did this.

Hissing sounds fill the air, followed by massive thuds.

THUNK! THUNK! THUNK!

Three lava angels fall from the sky, landing in a trio around Walker. As I'd hoped, the rain solidified their lava forms into rock. That won't last for long, though. Even a huge rainstorm won't stop molten magma for long.

Racing forward, Lincoln scoops up Walker.

"Canopic." Walker reaches toward the ground. "Jar."

My brows lift. That's right. Walker walk holding something. "I got it." I grab a glass jar from the ground, hold it against my chest like a football, and haul ass. Lincoln keeps pace beside me, despite the fact that he's carrying Walker. Rain pelts mercilessly. The ground turns slick.

Behind us, crackling sounds erupt. The angels are adjusting to the rain. I'd hoped for more time, but at least we have Walker and a chance for the gate.

The archway to Black Wing Manor appears before us. Rain drips into my eyes. It's getting harder to keep my grip on the glass jar. I race forward, Lincoln at my side.

The crackling noises behind us get louder. Heat sears into my back. The lava angels are chasing us. They're getting closer. The gate looms larger.

Twenty yards away.

Ten.

Five.

A molten hand grips my shoulder. Using my demonic strength, I leap forward and past the archway. Lincoln and Walker do the same beside me. We land in a roll on the manor grounds.

Safe.

I rise. Every inch of me is soaked in rain and covered in mud. Lincoln, Walker, Happy, and Jaime rush inside the manor. As they step inside, Happy's rainstorm vanishes. The fog reappears, but it doesn't stop my view of the lava angels. For some reason, I can only stare at those molten creatures on the other side of the gate. Their bodies have more of a grayish tinge, but they still glow red with heat and hate.

"Renounce this," says Inferno. "Prepare yourself for the inevitable and we'll let you live, *Mother Scala*." She slams her sword against the barrier. Fresh sparks arc into the air. "This won't last long. Enough swords against this barrier will slice it in two. We shall raise the Brimstone Legion, break into Black Stone Manor, and free Lucifer. It's all a matter of time."

I give her my back and head into the manor. Our side has Walker, Drayden, and about fifteen hours left. That may not be a ton of time, but we still have a lot left in terms of fight. That will have to do.

CHAPTER 20

A half hour has passed since we brought Walker into Black Wing Manor. My honorary brother lays shivering atop a small cot. The room is simple, just some dark wood floors and a simple bed by the wall. The place is nothing special, save for the fact that the chamber was near the front door.

Over the last thirty minutes, Lincoln has used every healing charm he carried in his armor. Nothing has worked. Right after we arrived, Jaime went off in search of Obsidian. The seraphim's a mage; maybe he can help. Since then, there's been no sign of either Jaime or Obsidian. That said, it's a massive mansion. Hopefully Jaime can find Obsidian soon.

Happy leans against a nearby wall. Like all of us, she's soaked to the skin. Her gaze stays locked on Walker. Tears mix with the rain dripping from her hair.

For my part, I've spent the last half hour kneeling beside Walker's cot, holding his hand. I've never felt him so cold. With each passing minute, despair presses in more tightly around me. Walker looks so hurt and miserable. Clearly, someone was torturing him, yet he escaped and found us.

And we've done nothing to heal him.

Lincoln stands over Walker. My guy's face is pale with worry. Reaching into his pocket, Lincoln pulls out his last healing charm. This one is camouflaged to look like a small purple pill. Leaning over the bed, Lincoln sets the small round charm into Walker's mouth.

"Come on, Walker," whispers Lincoln. "You can do this."

The pill bursts with purple light. Violet haze wafts up rom Walker's lips. Happy, Lincoln, and I all stare at our friend, hoping for some change.

Walker lays unmoving. The spell didn't help.

Jaime rushes through the door, breathless. "I found him."

Obsidian stomps into the room, his staff gripped tightly in his fist. Lowering his head, Obsidian begins murmuring something in a language I can't understand. Not a shocker. Lucas uses strange tongues in his spells all the time.

Hope sparks in my chest. Obsidian is a powerful mage. Perhaps he can do something.

A moment later, Obsidian's staff changes. The raven head atop the rod transforms. The bird's eyes glow with inhuman light. Opening its mouth, the enchanted raven lets out a loud caw. Red tendrils of misty power twist out of its beak, winding their way over to Walker.

As Obsidian continues his spell, the mists from his staff whirl around Walker's body. The tendrils become thick as mummy wrappings. Another flash of light follows as the cords of Obsidian's spell seep straight into Walker's body. The crow head atop the seraphim's rod returns to being a carving once more.

Obsidian raises his head and looks around the room. "I've cast a spell to give Walker more strength to heal. This magic isn't instantaneous. We won't know for hours if it works." The seraphim steps closer to the bed. "Walker has the power to heal. These wounds should be gone by now."

"It's the Viper," I explain. "For months, that fiend has been attacking Walker with Lucifer's Gauntlets. It leaves his powers weakened." A chill runs over my skin and it has nothing to do with the rain or cold. "The Viper broke into this mansion with portal power from Walker himself."

A thought appears in my mind. *Portal power. Is that the only thing the Viper stole from Walker?*

Snapping up my head, I meet Lincoln's gaze. That *chess playing look* has returned to his eyes.

"Are you thinking what I'm thinking?" asks Lincoln.

"Yes." I answer. "This is about more than portals."

Happy folds her arms over her chest. "You two need to stop speaking in code."

I can't help but crack a smile. "We thought the Viper was only stealing Walker's ability to create portals. But it's more than that. The Viper was after Walker's ability to heal."

Lincoln nods. "That's why the Viper kept attacking Walker, over and over. He'd drain the power to heal, but that magic is unique. It would replenish again."

Happy rushes over and picks up the canopic jar. "This thing stores magic, right?"

We all stare at the jar for a long minute. "I bet it storing some of Walker's healing power."

"Can we put it back in Walker?" asks Happy.

"Sadly, no," replies Lincoln. "We need Lucifer's Gauntlet to put it back inside him." He looks to Obsidian. "Is that something you can do?"

"Perhaps," replies Obsidian. "If I had a room full of canopic jars and a month to experiment. No seraphim has ever cast a spell like that before."

"In order words," says Happy. "That would be a no."

I tap my cheek. "There's more to this. Something we're missing. The Viper didn't steal Walker's powers so many times without a reason." I round on Obsidian. "What could the Viper want Walker's powers for?"

"I'm not sure," says Obsidian slowly. "But I know where you

can find more information." He turns to Happy. "You must finish your tour of the grounds. I'll go with you this time. It was a mistake for me to have stayed behind before."

"Happy's about to show how all the seraphim perished," says Jaime. "Anyone would understand why you wouldn't want to see that again."

I pull on my ear. *Not sure I heard that right.* "You're about to show us how the seraphim died?"

"Happy will show you, yes," answers Obsidian. "And I will accompany you. It's far less likely that any lava angels will attack if I'm with you."

"Less likely?" says Happy. "Works for me. Besides, I love punching Inferno in the face. Let's do this."

"I'll stay behind with Walker," says Jaime.

That buzzing feeling comes back to my chest. *My phone!* I pull out the device and see Cissy's name on the screen. I take call button while following Obsidian, Happy and Lincoln out the door.

"Myla, is that you?" Wherever Cissy is, there's a lot of shouting and background noise.

"Yes, are you on the Senate floor?" *No one shouts like Senators.*

"No, I'm at Enmity Farms with Zeke," says my bestie. "I don't want to freak you out, but…" I can't see Cissy, but I know my girl. She's worrying her lower lip with her teeth.

"Go on, Ciss. I can take it like a girl."

"The Enmity guys walled themselves up in the house. Shot-guns are sticking out the windows and everything. Oh, and there's smoke coming from the fireplace. I think they might be destroying evidence. We're about to raid the place." Muffled shouting sounds in the background. "Oh, I better go."

"Stay safe," I say. "Call me when you can."

The line goes dead.

Ugh. If Zeke and Cissy get murdered on a worm farm, I will never forgive myself.

CHAPTER 21

a few minutes later, our small group stands at the same spot where Happy cast her spell and revealed the graveyard. Happy turns to Obsidian. "How far back should I go?"

"Take them to the time Lucifer fell. Only please, do not make it real as you did the rain."

Happy raises her right brow. "Creating visions from the past takes energy. But adding in an actual physical element? That stings like Hell, so it's only for rare occasions. And for visions that don't include, you know…"

A major battle.

My pulse speeds. Not sure I want to see Obsidian's friends die. But if it helps us save Walker and Drayden? I'm all for it.

Happy rubs her hands together in a slow rhythm. Bits of white lightning flash between her palms. Kneeling down, Happy places her hands against the ground. "I cast my spell. Return this land to the time Lucifer fell."

More light bursts out from under Happy's palms. Once again, the power moves in a circle, reaching out across the grounds. For a moment, I see the same sight as before: a graveyard as far as the eye can see. Countless statues reaching off into infinity. I hug my elbows. Perhaps each grave marker symbolizes someone Lucifer killed.

How awful.

On reflex, I move closer to Lincoln. Wrapping his heavy arm around my waist, my guy pulls me against his side. It helps to feel his warmth and strength.

The image of the graveyard stays before us for a moment more. Then it disappears. The ground is empty and clear of fog. Stars twinkle in a clear sky. Above our heads, hundreds of angels fly in intricate circles. All of them wear silver armor and hold swords in their fists.

And none of them are molten.

This is the Brimstone Legion as they lived.

A shiver rocks across my shoulders. We're seeing the past. Before, Happy's magic took Inferno back to when the angel was twelve years old. Now happy is returning Black Wing Manor to the day Lucifer fell. Dad's story reappears. My father had promised to meet Lucifer on the field of battle for a formal challenge. Lucifer arrived with his Brimstone Legion so they could watch my father fall.

We're in the past.

The Brimstone Legion flies overhead.

This is the day that battle was supposed to take place.

I carefully scan Happy. The young girl who kneels against the earth, her eyes closed, power pulsing out from her hands. Indeed, this Chosen One is strong.

While the Brimstone Legion flies overhead, a new figure stomps toward us across the ground. Lucifer. There's no missing the golden hair, wings, and armor. Lucifer pauses some yards before us. His blue eyes flare with blue light.

On reflex, my tail arches over my shoulder, getting into battle stance. I pat the arrowhead shaped end. "He can't see us," I explain. "This isn't real. At least, not this time. We're watching shadows of the past." My tail scans from left to right and remains in battle stance. It so doesn't believe me on this one.

Lucifer leans back on his heels and bellows. "I invoke my right to a challenge an archangel duel. Xavier! Where are you?"

I lean more closely into Lincoln's side. This is what my father spoke about back in Purgatory. Dad tricked Lucifer here, to this very battlefield, saying that they would fight to the death.

"Come out, Xavier. Show yourself. One of us dies today."

Above our heads, the angels still swirl and dive in an intricate rhythm. It would be a beautiful dance, if it weren't for the silver swords and deadly intent.

Another figure steps forward, or to be accurate, it walks right through us. It's Obsidian, or a younger version of him. *Interesting.* Since this is a representation of the past, the seraphim must be able step right through those of us who are flesh and blood today.

Young Obsidian pauses. In some ways, he's the same as the Obsidian of today. The young version wears the same black armor and carries the identical staff. There are differences, though. Young Obsidian has a spring and purpose to his step. This isn't the same person who now bellows orders at Black Wing Manor.

"Greetings, King of the Angels," says Obsidian. "I come to tell you that none of the archangels will fight you in a duel today. Instead, we seraphim will finish you."

Lucifer's face brightens into a blazing smile. I mean, I've never seen anything so beautiful. It's the kind of joy that makes you want to follow him around, do his laundry, pay off his credit cards, anything to keep him close.

"Obsidian, my friend," says Lucifer. "The only way to kill me is by ritual combat, one to one, archangel to archangel. And even if you survive that, my Brimstone Legion flies overhead. Inferno, my Champion, is with them. Don't waste your life needlessly."

Eight more figures step forward. They are all seraphim, like Obsidian. Each one carries a staff.

Lucifer's smile grows wider. "So all nine of you will risk your lives. Please don't."

Young Obsidian lowers his head. A low murmur escapes his lips. *Another spell.* Wisps of red power curl out from Young Obsidian's staff. The raven head atop the stick comes to life and caws.

The other seraphim follow suit. Soon the air fills with their murmured spells. Fresh caws sound as their staffs come to life. I'm so fascinated by the seraphim before me, that it takes me a moment to notice that in the past, the scenery behind them has changed.

In the past, there's no gate protecting Black Wing Manor.

A chill runs through my veins. Not sure why that realization makes my hair stand on end, but it does.

Lucifer's mouth thins to an angry line. He rounds on the young version of Obsidian. "What is this? Do you really think some little spell of yours can kill me? I'm Lucifer, King of the Angels."

Moving in unison, the other seraphim take their staffs and lower them into the ground. A great flash of red light bursts from their bodies. Tendrils of power flash out toward Black Wing Manor. I saw this effect before when Obsidian tried to heal Walker. Instead of surrounding Walker, those red bands of power now surrounding Black Wing Manor, encasing the structure in a dome of crimson magic and light.

Lucifer raises his hand. "Angels, to me!"

Now, my father and I like to chat up battle strategy. According to Dad, battle strategy is nothing without soldiers who follow orders and fast. With that in mind, I have to admit one thing. The Brimstone Legion is an impressive fighting force. Lucifer says three words and they speed back in his direction, still keeping in their neat lines.

The seraphim smash their staffs down again. Fresh tendrils of red power shoot out once more. This time, the crimson magic of the seraphim encompasses Lucifer. Great ribbon-style loops of energy wind around the King of the Angels. Raising his golden sword, Lucifer strikes his weapon at the threads of energy. The golden blade slides harmlessly through.

"A charming party trick," says Lucifer. "But as you know, truly great magic requires a sacrifice to match. I came here for a duel to the death. You could all kill yourselves with a spell, yet your magic would never be enough to destroy me." He gestures behind him to the Brimstone Legion. The angelic warriors stand in neat rows that stretch off toward the horizon. "And even if you did succeed in destroying me, the Brimstone Legion would remain. Fly away, little birds. This is no place for you."

In reply, the seraphim thus down their staffs for a third time. Now the threads of crimson energy flash and roll beyond Lucifer.

Obsidian steps forward. "We don't plan to kill you or the Brimstone Legion. But destroy you all? That we will do. And the price will gladly be paid."

A chorus of moans sounds from the Brimstone Legion. For the first time, a look of mild alarm lights up Lucifer's eyes. The king of the Angels glances over his shoulder. The red ribbons of seraphim power now wind around each angelic warrior. As the energy soaks into their bodies, the angels transform. Wings turn solid. Arms freeze in place. Metal armor changes into stone. The warriors break rank as they try to run. There's nowhere to go.

Soon, the entire Brimstone Legion is transformed into stone angels.

A sick feeling twists inside me. That was no graveyard I saw before. At least, it wasn't a typical one. What I thought were grave markers were actual angels transformed into pale rock.

Some of the angels closest to Lucifer can still move. A dozen crawl and hobble toward him. Their cries echo across the grounds.

Help us!

Save us!

Lucifer doesn't seem to hear them. One angel scrambled close enough to grasp Lucifer's ankle. The King of the Angels kicks him away.

Wow. That's some cold shit, right there.

With his golden sword held high, Lucifer stalks toward Young Obsidian. However, at one time the King of the Angels strode with grace. Now his movement are stilted and slow. No question why, either. Lucifer is turning to stone as well. With each step closer to Obsidian, Lucifer speaks one word.

"Not … stone … for … long!"

By the time Lucifer reaches the word *stone*, his body becomes frozen in place. Where once was gold, now everything is now mottled shade of gray.

Young Obsidian shakes his head. "You don't have to stay stone forever," says Young Obsidian. "I only need time to imprison you in the seraphim's labyrinth."

Behind Obsidian, the other seraphim slam their staffs onto the ground once more. Before, the seraphim had sent bands of crimson energy to create a dome over Back Wing Manor. Now, more power tendrils speed toward the manor than ever before. As the dome around the manor grows brighter, the seraphim themselves change.

The seraphim's bodies begin to disintegrate. Only Obsidian remains whole. With a gasp, I realize what's happening. The Seraphim are putting their own life power into this final stage of the spell. The physical seraphim disappear as a tall gate forms around Black Wing manor. For a moment, the images of the seraphim glow red in the iron that creates the massive gate and fence. After that, the structure turns dark.

Young Obsidian races over to the new gate and fence. His blue eyes are lined with tears. "Thank you, my brothers and sisters. You sacrifice saves us all"

Magic has a price, and great magic has a steep price. To turn

Lucifer and his Brimstone Legion into stone—and to protect the prison inside Black Wing Manor—eight seraphim transformed into iron. They are literally the power that protects and encircles Back Wing Manor.

Young Obsidian kneels before the new iron fence, his shoulders heaving with sobs.

The current version of Obsidian speaks. "I lost my brothers and sisters that day. They have all been transformed, just as the Brimstone Legion. I can never have them back." He walks over to Happy and gently touches her shoulder. "It is over. They have seen what they need."

Happy lifts her hands from the ground. Her face glistens with sweat. Obsidian helps her to stand. Happy looks between me and Lincoln.

"Please tell me that help."

"It did," I say. "Thank you." The visions form the past combine with the present. Information aligns. Fractured facts weave into a greater tapestry. "I believe I now know what the Viper plans to do."

"And what's that?" asks Happy.

"The Viper's been draining Walker's powers for months, storing up that healing ability in canopic jars. Using Lucifer's Gauntlets, the Viper placed Walker's ability to heal inside one of the angels of the Brimstone Legion."

Happy frowns. "But they're all dead."

"I see what you mean, Myla." Lincoln focuses on Happy. "Take Inferno as an example. Was she dead? Perhaps that was true at one time. However, Walker's power is one of a kind. When his unique magic combined with the seraphim spell that froze Inferno, Walker's power healed her stone body. It transformed rock into lava and created magma versions of the Brimstone Legion."

Obsidian pounds his leg with his fist. "The Viper has been doing more than stealing into Black Wing Manor. Once that fiend got the ability to create a ghoul portal, he must have come out to the stone army to experiment with the gauntlets. All the Viper would need to do is portal to this spot, pull out power from a canopic jar, and put it inside a statue. That's how the Viper created Inferno under our very noses."

Lincoln scans the now foggy rounds. "The Viper must plan to reanimate all the Brimstone Legion. After that, he could attack Black Wing Manor and free Lucifer."

Happy turns to Obsidian, her eyes wide with fear. "That can't work, can it? We have the gate of seraphim to protect us, don't we?"

"Even the powers of the seraphim have limits." Obsidian hangs his head. "With thousands of molten angels cutting into the gate at once? Its magic would eventually shatter under that assault."

At that moment, my cell vibrates against my chest once more. I pull out the device and flip it open.

"Myla?" It's Cissy's. And her voice quivers in terror.

I suck in a shaky breath. This is exactly what I feared.

Enmity Farm has brought trouble to Cissy and Zeke.

CHAPTER 22

"*M*yla? Are you there?" Cissy's voice quickly accelerates from *downright scared* to *super hysterical.*

At this point, Lincoln leans his head closer to mine so we can both hear the conversation. Some of the tension loosens from my shoulders. I won't lie; it helps to have Lincoln's strength and warmth a little closer. I'm on a freaked-out phone call … in a foggy Goth sort-of graveyard … after seeing a reenactment of an entire army of angels getting transformed into stone (among other scary things). If I still had a binky and a blanket, I'd want those close too.

A few yards away, Obsidian and Happy wait semi-patiently. The two of them make quite a pair. There's the towering seraphim in his dark metal armor. Triple wings arch slightly behind his back. Beside Obsidian, there stands a twelve-year-old girl in a wet bustle-gown from the 1800s. Both stare at me and Lincoln with wide eyes. The words are there, if unspoken.

You're taking a phone call now? Really?

I totally get it. There's nothing like an odd phone call at the big moment. And this time is a doozy: we're deciding how to destroy the Viper and take down Lucifer. But Ciss wouldn't call unless it was urgent.

I raise my pointer finger, mouth the words *one minute*, and refocus on the phone. "It's me, Ciss. What's wrong? Is there a shootout at the farm?"

"That? No!"

"Good. Then did something turn up on Walker's watch?"

"No, there's been no word on that. Lucas is still doing his thing. No, I'm calling about the Enmity brothers outside of firearms. I screwed up. Something seemed off with them, but my agents thought it would just take time to develop them as contacts. The Enmity Boys knew everybody who was anybody, Myla. I should have sent someone in their farmhouse a long time ago."

"That's okay, just calm down and tell me what happened." My pulse speeds. "Are you sure that you and Zeke okay?"

"We're fine. We finally got into the house, though. You won't believe what we found inside. The place is full of books. It's all the stuff they showed on *Good Morning Purgatory:* super rare tomes on magic, angels, and all sorts of stuff. We found something else, too. *Walker's ring.* You know, the silver one with the book carved on it? Do you think someone brought Walker here?"

A shiver rolls down my back. When I last saw Walker in Purgatory, he was wearing that very ring. He even offered it to me before he left to save Drayden. A foul taste creeps into my mouth. All this time, Walker may have been in the Enmity brothers farm, being tortured.

Unholy Hell.

My thoughts race through the implication. Were the Enmity brothers just buddies with the Viper, or were they actively helping that fiend? The image of Walker's many wounds appears in my mind. That was serious torture. It's hard to imagine one of my own people going after Walker in that way.

But it is possible.

Rage and sorrow tighten my chest. "Do I think someone brought Walker there? I sure do."

"Oh," continues Cissy. "They have all these canopic jars lying around. And journals. So many journals! All of them are covered in notes like 'extracted gluttony magic, no change to the angels.' Do you think that's related to Inferno?"

"Yup." My mouth pops on the 'P' sound. "The Viper was trying to find out what kind of magic would bring back the Brimstone Legion. Are the brothers there? Did you question them? I think they know who the Viper is." *Or worse.*

"That's the thing, Myla. The brothers are gone." Cissy lowers her voice. "My people think they used ghoul portals to get away. So I thought about what you said back at your parents' house. The Viper stole the ability to create portals from some unsuspecting ghouls. If all the Enmity brothers portalled away, then what does that mean?"

A new voice sounds nearby, breaking up our conversation. Familiar words echo through the heavy mist.

"Hello, Scala Mother."

My heart tumbles to my feet. I know that voice.

It's Travis Enmity.

CHAPTER 23

I stand outside the Black Wing Manor. My mind takes a snapshot of the moment. Lincoln and I stand with our heads touching as we listen to Cissy's call. Mist surrounds us. Somewhere in that heavy fog there lay thousands of angels from the Brimstone Legion, all of them frozen into stone. Obsidian and Happy wait a few yards away. Their faces have turned from looks of mild of curiosity to downright alarm.

Those fateful words sound again. "Hello, Scala Mother."

Back on the phone, Cissy raises her voice. "Did you hear what I said?" she asks. "The Enmity brothers used portals to escape. What does that mean?"

I choke out one word. "Trouble."

Cissy gasps. "Are you okay?"

A hum sounds as a ghoul portal opens before me and Lincoln. A moment later, Trav steps out of the black door-shaped hole, pulls the phone off my neck, and crushes the device in his hand. The portal vanishes behind him.

I glare at him. "I wasn't done with that call."

"How about *we* talk instead?" asks Trav. His outfit has certainly changed. Instead of jeans and a t-shirt, Trav now wears purple body armor. It's the same stuff that Zeke uses with his guards. Which solves another mystery.

That's the armor which went missing months ago.

Trav raises his hands. Golden bracers now cover his arms from his elbow to wrist. The metal is decorated in a pattern of angel wings.

Words fall from my mouth. "You're wearing Lucifer's Gauntlets."

Trav bows slightly at the waist. "I donned them in your honor."

"Okay." *Eew.*

From my peripheral vision, I catch Obsidian lowering his head. The raven on his staff comes to life, its beak opening in a silent caw. *Obsidian is casting a spell.* Most likely, the seraphim is scanning our new guests. After all, that's what Obsidian did when Lincoln and I first arrived.

Beside me, Lincoln shifts his weight slightly. No need to glance his way. I already know what Lincoln's up to. My guy is subtly pulling his baculum from their holster. Warmth and love warm my chest.

Always battle ready. That's my Lincoln.

"I did all this for you, Scala Mother." Trav frowns. "Doesn't it please you?"

How can he ask that question? "You're the Viper."

"Is that what you think?" Trav cups his hand by his mouth. "Brothers!"

A chorus of hums sound as six more portals open nearby. The remaining Enmity brothers step onto the grounds. Like Trav, they all wear the purple armor of the Senatorial guard. Each also carries a canopic jar and a seriously grouchy attitude. The portal door holes silently vanish.

It's official. This situation now qualifies as a little something I like to call: *oh shit.*

"The Viper isn't one person." Trav gestures across his brothers. "My brothers and I all work together to form the Viper. We're worms with fangs, you might say."

"Clever," deadpans Lincoln.

Obsidian steps forward. "Trespassers! Thieves!" The veins on his neck pulse with rage. "My spells just uncovered the truth. You poisoned Drayden."

After that, things happen so fast, it's hard to keep track. Obsidian raises his staff while murmuring a fresh spell. This time, the crow end caws with fury. Happy rubs her palms together and kneels. That's another spell a-coming, right there. Lincoln ignites his baculum into a long sword. Adrenaline pumps through my veins.

Trav stares at me, cool as anything. "Don't make me raise the Brimstone Legion. I don't want to kill your friends."

The Enmity brothers raise their canopic jars high. All their eyes are locked on Trav.

"I'm not attacking you, Scala Mother." In a gesture of peace, Trav raises his arms with his palms forward. "We only want to talk."

Obsidian's murmuring grows louder. Happy's voice echoes across the clearing. "I cast my spell," she begins.

"What did you say to Inferno at the grain bin? She told me all about it." Trav lowers his voice. "'Come on,' you said. 'Make the first move.' I know my Scala Mother. You don't strike unless someone else attacks first."

I raise my hands. "Everyone stop. Trav and his people aren't assaulting us."

Happy and Lincoln pause. Obsidian? Not so much. The seraphim slams his staff on the ground. "I will not stand down. These men poisoned Drayden."

"And they're also holding enough canopic jars of power to light up the entire Brimstone League. You want thousands of Infernos raiding Black Wing Manor, or should we listen to what the Viper Brothers have to say?"

A long moment follows while Obsidian scans the faces of the Enmity boy. The seraphim slams his staff onto the ground once more. The crow head returns to being a carving. Crisis temporarily avoided. Go me.

I focus on Trav. "See that?" I gesture toward Obsidian's staff. "The seraphim has stopped casting spells. Everyone else is standing down. I'm ready to listen to what you have to say."

"Thank you, Scala Mother." Trav runs his fingertips over the feather pattern on one arm of Lucifer's Gauntlets. "The Viper Brothers." He keeps petting his arm. "I like that name." At last, Trav stops petting his arm. "For all of history, Purgatory has been nothing but an afterthought. And yet we perform the most crucial service of any after-realm. What do ghouls offer anyone? Nothing. Angels sit on clouds and keep to themselves. Antrum and thrax are necessary, but only because no one has ever finished the job of cleaning out Hell. So who should be the real power in the after-realms?" He stares at me.

I know what Trav wants me to say—namely that quasis should rule everyone—but there's no way those words are leaving my lips.

Which brings me to a crossroads.

Normally, I'd counter with some snark. But my goal here is to negotiate peace without thousands of magma angels flying around and a psychopathic Lucifer on the loose.

In the end, I decide to play dumb. "Who do you think should be ruling?"

Trav raises his fist. "The quasis."

Surprise, surprise.

"We should be the new power in the after-realms," continues Trav. "You're a key part of that, don't you see? The Viper Brothers. Our Scala Mother. We're all one family."

Ick.

Trav reaches out to cup my cheek. The movement is like watching a bowl of ice cream tumble toward the kitchen floor.

You see it happening, but are powerless to stop it. In this case, there's no yummy ice cream. Instead, thick fingers head toward my face.

Gah.

Quick as lightning, Lincoln steps between me and Trav. "Back off," orders my guy.

Trav lifts his hands in a gesture that says, *I wasn't doing anything.*

Sure, you weren't.

"Go farther away," commands Lincoln.

Trav glares at Lincoln for a hot minute, and then takes a pointed step backward. "Is this good enough?" asks Trav. There's no small amount of sarcasm in the quasi's voice.

"For now," replies Lincoln.

"See?" Trav turns to me. "I don't want to hurt you or your Consort. And the Scala Heir is our sacred little brother. In fact, I even hated ruining your phone. Anything you touch is a holy relic. I've wanted to convince you of things, but I wasn't sure how to go about it. So I've sent Inferno to talk to you. Since you're an archangel's daughter, I thought Inferno might be more goddess-like and impressive."

Oooookay. We're all still talking and not raising lava angel armies, so I should really let that Inferno comment slide.

Don't be snarky. Don't be snarky. Don't be snarky.

Screw it. I'm being snarky.

"Inferno was not goddess-like and impressive. More like a molten marshmallow you can't get off your thumb."

"Inferno will arrive soon." Trav scans the skies. "I'll deal with her then. It's unacceptable to displease our Scala Mother."

I nod. My little bit of snark seems to have landed well. No war and Inferno's in the dog house. *Nice.*

"Since Inferno failed," continues Trav, "allow me to convince you."

Not sure I like where this conversation is going.

"Convince me of what?" I ask.

"Why, once I take on Lucifer's powers, I'll be King of the Angels. I want you to be my queen."

Every nerve ending in my body goes on alert.

Eew, eew, eew.

"Dang." Wincing, I make *'my gee wiz what a shame'* face. "Thanks for the offer, but I'm already a queen."

"You rule the thrax," counters Trav. "That doesn't count."

"It does to me," says Lincoln. Muscles flex in his neck. My guy is close to losing it.

For the record, Lincoln deserves an award for not ripping Trav's head off. My husband is downright territorial when it comes to me.

"Please," says Trav. "I won't touch you or anything like that."

I raise my pointer finger. "You tried to do that a minute ago."

Trav laughs like I made a joke. "It will all be a show for our people. The quasis need to see a continuation of leadership. You, your mother, your father. If we all agree that the quasis must rule over everyone with me as King of the After-Realms, then the transition will go much easier."

I rub my neck and think things through. This isn't some dumb ass thief who wants to just grab Lucifer's power and steal more stuff. Nope. Trav has a plan. Which brings me to my next question.

"And if I disagree?"

Trav points to a nearby canopic jar. "We can do it the hard way. Raise the Brimstone Legion." Setting his pinkies on either side of his mouth, Trav lets out an ear-piercing whistle. "Inferno!" he cries.

Red lights flicker in the skies above. Waves of heat cascade around us. Fog billows as Inferno lands nearby. She turns to Trav. "Yes, Your Highness?"

"Once I raise the Brimstone Legion, how long before your angels break down the gates of Black Wing Manor?"

"About seven minutes."

"And overrun the after-realms?"

"Once you take in Lucifer's power, only a matter of days. With our new molten forms, we can cause far more damage."

Trav focuses on me again. "Do you really want to be responsible for so much carnage?"

I pinch the bridge of my nose. "You're assuming all this will work. To begin with, Lucifer won't let you drag out his powers. Plus, my parents will never allow you to rule the after-realms, no matter what I say. You've cooked up a crackpot idea."

"How can you say such things?" Trav stomps his foot. "All the hard work has been done already by me. *I* was the one who found Lucifer's Gauntlets on our farm. I figured out how to use their power to make ghoul portals. I enabled my brothers to take what we wanted. First smaller heists, then bigger ones. In fact, we were so effective, your father built a Pulpitum near our farm. He thought demons were at work and thrax needed quick access. Imagine that. Demons!"

Trav taps his chest with his fist. "Your father and his Pulpitum gave me an idea. If someone like Xavier thinks I'm as powerful as a demon, what *can't* I do? So I snuck into the Dark Lands, got some books, and put together our master plan. What we needed was an army, and the books said there's one right here! After that, we had to figure out what kind of magic would raise the Brimstone Legion. We tried all sorts of powers, but ran across Walker's by accident. And Walker changed everything. With his magic, we raised Inferno, and then? Walker was a gift that kept on giving. Every time we'd drain him, his power would eventually return. In his honor, we even leaked information about our crimes to *Good Morning Purgatory* and gave Walker's name as the source."

"Keep talking about Walker and I'll punch you in the face."

Trav's mouth thins to an angry line. "I even deduced how to raise all the stone angels at once, only by using my brothers, canopic jars with Walker's power, and Lucifer's Gauntlets. So don't tell me my plan won't work. It already has. Now we're ready. It's your choice, Scala Mother. Will you lead our family in a bloodless war? Will you be my queen? Or must we do this the hard way?"

"Um…" I shift my weight foot to foot. "No."

Trav's scorpion tail arches over his shoulder. "I didn't want it to come to this."

"To what?"

"I can take your powers out with these gantlets, and then place them in someone else. I don't want to do that. But I'm to become become King of the After-Realms, then I've got hard choices ahead of me. I'll take care of my family first."

"Did you hear that?" asks Obsidian. "Talking to this criminal is pointless."

"Give me another minute here," I say. Obsidian frowns, but he doesn't turn his staff into a talking raven, either.

When I next speak, I take care to look across Trav and all the enmity Brothers. "I heard Trav's words. Now you all must listen to your Scala Mother." The seven brothers stare in my direction, their eyes large and mouths open.

I've got one shot at this. Come on, verbal fireworks.

"You've talked a lot about family," I begin. "Did you know there are four kinds? Family of the heart, of the mind, of the soul, and of the body. Indeed, we quasis are all family of the body in that we share tails and powers across the deadly sins. But what about the mind? Inside Black Wing Manor, there's a ghoul who wrote books on military strategy that saved the after-realms at the Battle of the Gates. That's family of the mind."

I scan the Enmity brother's faces. Trav looks unconvinced, but some of the other guys are nodding slightly. *It's working.*

"Then, there's Walker. Yes, he's a ghoul, but he serves us all selflessly. He built our new soul storage towers. Did you know that? No one does. Walker wouldn't let us put his name on the buildings. Whatever Walker does, he's a good man. That's family of the soul."

Now, almost all the Enmity brothers are nodding. *I'm getting there.*

"Then we get to heart. Here, I'll talk about my own father. Dad chose imprisonment in Hell to save my mother from Armageddon. He did this because he loved her, but there was more to it than that. Dad knew Mom could lead Purgatory out of ghoul rule. He sacrificed himself in part so Mom could realize that potential. And all of us benefit from that love every day. That's family of the heart."

The clearing becomes quiet. Anticipation hangs in the air. Even Inferno is watching me carefully.

"Knowing that, how can you only define family as one thing? Lincoln's my family. Walker's my family. You're my family. Families don't raise armies against each other because we think we've been treated poorly. Families work through problems with their heart, mind, and soul." I focus all my attention on Trav. "Now, what do you say?"

Trav stares into my eyes for a long minute. His features stay unreadable. Eons seem to eke by as I wait for his response.

"Brothers! Inferno!" Trav lifts his fist. "Raise the angels!"

My heart sinks to my toes.

Fuck fuck fuckity FUCK fuck.

CHAPTER 24

$\mathcal{T}$rav's words still ring in my ears. *Brothers! Inferno! Raise the angels!*

What happens next only takes a few seconds, but it unfolds much more slowly. It's that *ice cream falling off the table* situation again, only where there was once *ice cream*, now insert *evil molten angelic army.*

Moving in unison, all the brothers stomp on their canopic jars.

I gasp. *Stomping. What the WHAT?*

Trav said he figured out how the gauntlets could raise all of the Brimstone Legion at once. But he also said that he and his brothers spent months draining Walker of healing magic. All that power from Walker is now jammed into those canopic jars. I can't image how smashing them is a good thing.

Threads of blue power hover above the crushed remnants of the canopic jars. The thin cords twinkle with azure light. That's Walker's energy and it's beautiful. After stepping approaching a smashed jar, Trav sets his hands into the nest of power threads and raises his arms. The lines of blue magic in his palms glow more brightly.

"Inferno!" calls Trav. "Begin!"

While standing upright, Inferno pumps her molten wings in a steady rhythm. The threads react to the streams of air from her motion. Tiny blue cords unwind and fly across the field to where the stone angels lie. Wherever the lines of energy go, they clear out the fog and loop around the stone bodies. Quick as a heart-beat, the entire field of stone angels are connected by an intricate web of blue power strands. A thought occurs to me.

Walker is so powerful, he created enough magic for this. His angelic gift is incredible and unique. *What's it really for?*

The thought disappears as Trav lets out another cry. "Awaken!"

Bright blue light streams along all the threads connecting the field. A symphony of cracking noises sound as the angels begin to move. Molten red fissures appear along their bodies. Wings unfurl. Swords blaze.

The Brimstone Legion rises again.

Trav watches the scene, his chest puffed out in triumph. "See that?" he calls to me. "I tested this very scenario with Inferno and two angels before this day. That's how I plan. It's why I'll be King."

Inferno stalks up to Trav's side. "Thank you, Your Highness. You raised my brothers and sisters."

Raising her arm high, Inferno then drives her sword straight through Trav's chest. For a few heartbeats, Trav stares at Inferno. Blood drips from his chin as his mouth forms soundless words. Then he slumps over, dead.

Inferno pulls her sword from Trav's chest. "You have served Lucifer well."

Shock jolts down my spine. Gotta be honest here.

I did not see that coming.

CHAPTER 25

rav's body crumples onto the earth. Inferno towers over him. "I shall tell Lucifer of your great sacrifice," she says in a low voice. "And that of your friends as well."

Lincoln and I exchange a shocked look. *Your friends?*

While we were focused on Inferno and Trav, more lava angels have snuck up behind us. Heat burns into my back. An electric kind of awareness skitters over my skin.

They'll soon attack.

My inner wrath demon instantly awakens. Energy and power spin through my mind. My *battle sense* kicks in and how. Time appears to slow as I soak in my surroundings. Lava angels now loom behind me, Lincoln, Happy, Obsidian, and all the remaining Enmity brothers.

"Everyone down!" cries Lincoln.

Happy, Obsidian, and I all heed Lincoln's warning. Fast as a heartbeat, we crouch low to the ground. A whoosh sounds above me as a molten sword swipes over my head. Pulling out my baculum, I ignite them into short swords, stand, spin about, and go to town.

My blades crisscross before me as I slice through the lava

angel assigned to end my life. Rage consumes me. Who gets their army raised from the dead and then kills who helped them? Sure it was a dumb idea to revive the Brimstone Legion, but more death is not the right response. My temper snaps.

Swipe.

That's for Drayden.

Swipe.

That's for Walker.

Swipe.

That's for me.

Soft pressure lands on my shoulder. Looking over, I see Lincoln at my side. "I think you got him," he says dryly.

Looking down, I find my lava angel is diced up into mush. "Got a little carried away there, huh?"

"I gave you a minute to let off some steam, but it was starting to get awkward."

Stepping back, I scan my surroundings once more. The only folks left standing are Obsidian, Happy, Lincoln, and me. Nearby, there lay a lot of dead Enmity brothers. *Oops.*

"What did I miss?"

Happy shrugs. "The Enmity brothers didn't duck."

A weight settles into my heart. Sure, I ran across the Enmity brothers after they'd cooked up their *'let's rule the after-realms'* plan, but what if they'd never turned up Lucifer's Gauntlets in the first place? The Enmity boys could have been model citizens. As Mom says, when it comes to power, some people shouldn't be tempted.

"What happened to the lava angels?" I ask.

"Obsidian and I took down the other angels. Inferno then called for the angels to get back in ranks." Lincoln lets out a low whistle. "And these warriors follow orders to the letter. Once our angels reformed, they took off for the skies. Yours will do the same once it's back together." Lincoln purses his lips. "That might take a while, though."

Leaning back on my heels, I scan the heavens. Thousands of lava angels fly in neat formations. At this distance, their bodies paint the clouds in shifting layers of sunset red. As the warriors fly about, they stay grouped into neat columns that arc and twist through each other like ribbons.

Inferno's voice booms down from above. "Brothers and sisters! We must break into Black Wing Manor and free Lucifer!"

Again, it strikes me how well trained these warriors are. The Brimstone Legion gets zapped into stone for thousands of years, raised up into molten form, and then—*BOOM!*—there's no fuss. They heed orders and follow Inferno's plan to attack Black Wing Manor.

Speaking of battle plans, I need one of my own. Once more, my mind slows as I consider my options and inspect my surroundings. Overhead, the skies shift with crimson light as thousands of lava angels circle Black Wing Manor. Happy stands nearby, hugging her elbows. Obsidian waits at her side, his face pale with shock. The Enmity brothers lay lifeless on the ground.

Yup. I can work with this.

Lincoln glances at me over his shoulder. Everything confident and calm shines in his mismatched eyes. "What've you got for me?"

I wink. "Who says I have anything?"

"I do. You've had all of two minutes to come up with a plan."

"We have one key advantage." I point at Trav's dead body. "Guess what Inferno left behind?"

A slow smile winds Lincoln's mouth. "Lucifer's Gauntlets."

"Someone got a little over-excited to free her boss."

That *master chess player* look returns to Lincoln's face. "Plus, Walker had a canopic jar, remember? When I brought him inside, Walker told me the jar held his healing magic. We didn't yet have the gauntlets, so the jar wasn't useful at the time."

Obsidian scans the skies. "The lava angels won't stay up there for long. What's our next step?"

I march over to the very dead Trav. "I'll pull these gauntlets off Trav here. You get the canopic jar from Walker. Then we'll all meet at the gate surrounding Black Wing Manor."

Obsidian's face falls slack with shock. "You don't mean ... you can't ..."

"Oh, I totally can. Trav here was helpful enough to give a step-by-step demonstration of how to use six canopic jars and Lucifer's Gauntlets in order to raise thousands of lava angels. If we get one canopic jar, it should be more than enough to raise eight seraphim."

"My brothers and sisters." Obsidian takes a half step backward. "We were created as a flock."

"And soon you can fight as one again. Your fellow seraphim already know how to transform lava angels into a bunch of rocks, so let's make that happen."

Obsidian still stands there. Happy nudges him with her elbow. "You should get going. Besides, Jaime is with Walker. Someone should check on him."

The name *Jaime* gets Obsidian focused again and how. "Right." His triple sets of wings unfurl behind him. "I'll meet you at the gate." There's a lot of complex flapping noises and Obsidian takes off.

Someone taps my shoulder. It's Lincoln and if he wasn't the most amazing husband in the world before, he's officially winning an award. Why? My guy went and took Lucifer's Gauntlets off Trav's dead body. Now he hands them to me.

I scoop the gauntlets from Lincoln's hands. "Thank you so much."

Folks say that a romantic dinner with candlelight and champagne is the sign of true love. I disagree. In my opinion, if you find a guy who'll pick valuables off a dead body for you, that's a keeper.

With quick movements, I put the gauntlets onto my lower arms. The things are enchanted so they fit perfectly without a lot of fuss. *That's good design.* Lucifer: bloodthirsty psychopath and yet, talented armor designer. Who knew?

I do that scrunchy thing with my fingers to test the gauntlets out. "This will work. Let's head for the gate."

Happy frowns. "I see a problem with that."

"What?" asks Lincoln.

Happy points to the sky. The Brimstone Legion is now flying in a great loop around Black Wing Manor. The good news is that they aren't attacking the manor proper. At this point, they're circling the place in a modified donut-style formation. The bad news is the reason why they're circling in the first place.

Directly above the manor roof, Obsidian and Inferno are locked in aerial combat. She swoops at him with her magma sword. He tries blasting her with his magic.

"Neither have made a direct hits yet," says Lincoln. "This fight could last a while."

"Got it," I say. "So we can't rely on Obsidian to get the canopic jar. Time for Plan B."

"And what's plan B?" asks Lincoln.

"I'm working on it."

Lincoln scans the nearby grounds with an expert eye. "We shouldn't break up. None of us have the battle power of Obsidian. How about we hit the manor, grab the canopic jar, and then rush the gate?"

I nod my head, considering. "I like this plan."

Happy frowns once more. "I can see a problem with that. Again."

"And what's that?" I ask.

"You have two lava angels behind you."

Spinning about, I find none other than Charro 1 and Charro 2. "Hey," I say as casually as possible. "Aren't you two supposed to be flying in formation like Inferno asked?"

Moving in unison, they take out their molten swords.

"So, a few of us are carrying grudges. Noted. For the record, I didn't realize skewering you through the brain would be an owie."

Looking to Lincoln, I force a bright note into my voice. "Time for Plan C. We deal with these guys and then go to the manor. Before the angels attack. And Obsidian gets killed." I groan. "I'm really not liking this plan."

Happy perks up. "I have an idea. Keep the evil angels busy. I'll do my thing."

My father says that a good leader takes advice from people they respect, and I definitely respect Happy. "Let's do this."

The lava angels step closer; Lincoln and I ignite our baculum into long swords. The angels attack and we block their blades. Meanwhile, Happy rubs her palms together, kneels down, and sets her hands against the earth.

"I cast my spell," intones Happy. "Return this ground to when Walker came back to us."

White light spreads out from Happy's palms. The world around us changes. Once more, Walker lies on the ground. The same two angels stand off in the distance. This is a vision of the past where Charro 1 and 2 haven't found Walker yet.

Happy's face tightens with pain. "I'm making this one physical."

"Like you did with the rain?" I ask.

Happy nods. "Only doing this hurts like anything. So make it quick. Someone grab that canopic jar."

"What happens to the real canopic jar?" asks Lincoln.

"Nothing. I'm creating a magical copy. Doing this hurts like a psychic root canal, so can someone get it already?"

Stepping forward, I reach for the canopic jar. *Yes!* It's solid in my hands. "I got it."

Happy exhales. "Thank you." Her features turn peaceful. "Now the scene is just a vision again."

I turn over the small jar in my hands. Now, I have Lucifer's Gauntlets and a canopic jar loaded with Walker power.

Better for our side.

The scene Happy created vanishes with a flash of light. Once more, we're back on the battlefield before Black Wing Manor. Charro 1 and 2 took off, which is good news. I don't know what else happened while we were away with Happy's spell, but it seems like we missed something pretty big. The aerial battle with Obsidian and Inferno is now over. It isn't clear who won because there's no sign of either the seraphim or Lucifer's Champion. That said, all the lava angels in the Brimstone Legion are now flying in attack formation. Their target?

The magical gate surrounding Black Wing Manor.

No question what their plan is here. The Brimstone Legion want to shatter the gate, break into the manor, and free Lucifer. Like dive-bombing planes, the aerial warriors fly at the metal barrier. Once they near the iron, the angels strike the metal with their molten blades. The power of the seraphim repulse their attacks, but that magic won't last forever.

Already, sections of gate are wobbling under the relentless assault. The angels fly in a complex knot of lines, twisting and diving through each other before slashing the barrier with their swords.

The manor's defenses won't last much longer.

Worse for our side.

CHAPTER 26

L incoln, Happy, and I race toward the main gate for the Black Wing Manor. Overhead, lava angels continue to fly in their intricate formations. All their paths end with a sword-and-slash maneuver at the manor's gate. The barrier now shakes so much, the ground beneath trembles as well. Long metallic creaks fill the air.

The angels fly in low so they can slash at the gate. At the entrance archway, there's about three feet of clearance between the steady barrage of flying warriors and the ground.

Not a lot of room for sneaking in.

Odd things creep into your mind at times like these. For some reason, I think of this old human horror movie, *The Birds*. In it, a whole mass of *you-know-whats* swarmed people when they stepped outside. The scene before me is like that, only replace lava angels with birds and have them be super organized in their assault. And there's also magic, gauntlets, seraphim, and a super-natural preteen.

I take it back.

This is nothing like *The Birds*.

The three of us pause a short distance from the entrance

archway. The heavy mist provides come cover, but the angels could detect us if they tried.

"They aren't attacking," says Happy. "Why?"

"It's how things work in the angelic army," I explain. "Inferno is their commanding officer. She must have ordered them to attack the gate. They won't break rank unless they're close to death or have a personal vendetta." I glance over my shoulder. Speaking of personal vendettas, Charro 1 and 2 are still missing. *Bonus.*

Happy scans the skies. "Where's Inferno?"

"No idea," replies Lincoln. "And I still don't see Obsidian, either."

The gate rattles more violently. We don't have long.

"Let's make a run for the archway." Lincoln focuses on Happy. "Myla and I will keep you between us. When we say *down,* you go down."

"Got it," says Happy.

"On my mark." As Lincoln speaks, he leans over at the waist. Happy and I do the same.

"3, 2, 1!"

We all take off for the gate. The angels continue their assault. Long cracks form in the iron. Bits of filigree tumble to the ground.

When we're almost at the entrance archway, Lincoln cries one word. "Down!"

I grip Happy at the waist and twist her onto her side. Lincoln does the same. We all slam onto the ground. Our momentum keeps us moving under the archway. Inches above our heads, angels fly at the gate in ever-faster barrage.

We make it inside.

At that moment, great snaps of metal sound. Six huge sections of gate wobble, one for each seraphim who created the structure.

The gate tumbles over.

"No!" I roll over to the nearest slab of fallen iron, drop the canopic jar, and smash it under my boot. Blue threads of power wind up from the container. The thin cords twist and dance in the air right above the shattered glass. Just as Trav did, I grasp the glowing threads and shove them toward the nearest stretch of gate. I even use a version of what he said to the Brimstone Legion.

"Raise the angels! Awaken!"

Nothing happens.

The lava angels do one last set of swirls through the air before landing on the earth. They arrange themselves into a long row of warriors, about fifty across and stretching into the distance as far the eye can see. Moving in unison, the Brimstone Legion marches toward the front door of Black Wing Manor.

All that stands between them and the manor are me, Lincoln, Happy, and a bunch of broken up gates. Damn.

The Brimstone Legion stomps closer. But the lava angels aren't the only ones who move in unison. Together, Lincoln and I rise to stand. If the Brimstone Legion starts marching now, we both know they will never stop.

I pull out my baculum. The first line of warriors are only twenty yards away.

Ten.

Five.

"Look!" cries Happy. "The gate!"

It's a risk to take my gaze away from the battle, but I shoot a quick glance at the gate. It's transforming. The blue lines of Walker's power now wind around the fallen sections of metal. The slabs of iron shimmy, crackle, and burst. Any sign of the gate disappears. Now eight seraphim stand before us.

And they are completely formed from metal.

The seraphim raise their staffs high. Every rod still ends with a bird carving. The metal birds open their mouths, letting out a great series of caws. At the sound of his people, Obsidian comes rushing out of Black Wing Manor. Not sure where's he's been this whole time, but I'm super glad to see him now.

"My brothers and sisters!" calls Obsidian. "We must defeat the Brimstone Legion once more."

That's all Obsidian has to say. The seraphim round on the approaching army. Raising their staffs, they all murmur strange words in unison. My pulse skyrockets. The seraphim are alive. This simply has to work.

Tendrils of red power shoot out from the seraphim staffs and roll over the Brimstone Legion. As the crimson lines encircle the lava angels, their bodies slow. Lava bright lines fade to gray.

Lincoln pulls me against his side. "It's working, Myla!"

I wrap my arms around his waist. "I can't believe it!"

The red tendrils transform the lava angels to stone. Where once stood a crimson army, now lines of statues stretch off into the distance. With the Brimstone Legion transformed, the seraphim's power ricochets back into their staffs and bodies. Obsidian races to stand before them. "We know how to cure you now. I won't rest until you reawaken."

The red energy reenters the seraphim. Crimson light bursts around them, only this time, the seraphim aren't changed into a gateway. Instead, they remain as they were during the battle. Eight metal statues of seraphim now peer out over a landscape covered in stone angels.

Happy pumps her fist in the air. "We did it!"

Obsidian strides up to me and Lincoln. For once, the seraphim is all smiles. "You got the gauntlets. Brilliant!"

Pulling me into his arms, Lincoln spins me about before resetting me on the ground. "My girl has some serious skills." He kisses the tip of my nose. I'm tempted to take the kiss deeper when a familiar voice sounds from the manor stairs.

"Myla! Lincoln!"

It's Walker.

My honorary older brother hobbles his way down the front

steps with Jaime's help. Walker still looks half dead, but he's still carrying his canopic jar under his arm. Somewhere along the line, he got a loose pair of pants to wear. Jaime was probably behind that improvement. They look to be around the same size.

Walker pauses, scanning my lower arms. "Good! You're wearing Lucifer's Gauntlets. Now all you need is this." He lifts the canopic jar from under his arm.

"We're good. The Brimstone Legion is all rocked up again." I make shoo fingers at him. "Get back to bed."

Two more figures appear at the top of the steps. Every nerve ending in my body goes on alert.

It's Inferno and Lucifer.

And they both look pissed.

Hells Bells.

Inferno's lava body flares more brightly. "Foolish Obsidian. You shouldn't have stopped persuing me simply because your fellow birds let out a call. Look what I discovered after you left." She gestures to Lucifer.

Yeah, we see him all right. Damn.

Lucifer strides out from the doorway. Again, his supernatural beauty is striking. Combine that with some charisma? I get why Dad said *Luce could talk the cold off snow.*

"I am Lucifer, King of the Angels. I have escaped my prison and wish to finish the death duel I started so long ago. Are there any pureblood archangels here to fight me? Who accepts my challenge?"

Little by little, Walker turns to face Lucifer. "I do."

I can't have heard that right. Walker's in no shape to battle Lucifer.

But as always, my honorary older brother has ideas of his own. When he speaks again, Walker's voice is loud and strong.

"I said, I accept your challenge."

My mind speeds back to when I was twelve years old and entered the Arena for the first time. Is this how Walker felt when

I stepped out onto the floor? Did he wonder if I was walking to my death? Perhaps he did. But I needed his strength if I would ever succeed. After so many years, I know Walker well enough to realize one thing.

If he's promised to fight Lucifer, then that's what Walker will do.

Which means only one course of action remains to me.

I shoot him a hearty thumbs-up and call out in a loud voice:

"Kick his ass, Walker!"

CHAPTER 27

*J*f Lucifer hears my cry, he doesn't show it. Instead, the King of the Angels focuses on Walker. Lucifer's handsome face creases with confusion. "What did you say, ghoul?"

"I am WKR-7, descendant of Aquila. I accept your challenge. But I ask first to be healed."

Lucifer gives one of those combination sniff-and-chuckle things that are popular with truly arrogant people everywhere. "I'm a warrior, not a medic."

"I didn't ask for your help," says Walker. "I request the aid of Myla Lewis, daughter to the archangel Xavier and my personal physician."

Say what?

In that moment, I know why Walker is unique. Powerful. Brilliant. Fearless. And yes, it's in part due to his great soul. But it's something more. Walker's always held so many secrets. Something tells me I'm about to discover yet another one.

Plus, I've already decided to support Walker no matter what, so there's that.

I stroll over to Walker's side and make a great show of eyeing him up and down. "Yes, I can fix you quite easily. But I do need *my* assistant." I wave to Obsidian. "Boy! Come here!"

Obsidian stares at me, his brows pulled low. Clearly, elaborate hoaxes are not a popular part of seraphim culture.

Lucifer frowns. "Obsidian is your assistant's assistant?"

I look down my nose at Lucifer. "You've been locked up for two thousand years. How can you be shocked that a few social structures have changed? Dad says *hi*, by the way. He feels bad about tricking you into prison for a few millennia."

Kinda. Sorta. Not really.

Turning, I glare at Obsidian. "Over. Here. Now."

Lincoln raises his hand. "I'll help him."

"And who are you?" asks Lucifer.

"I'm the assistant's assistant's assistant." Lincoln grabs Obsidian by the elbow and guides him closer.

For her part, Inferno straightens her stance. "Permission to speak."

Lucifer gives her a dismissive wave over his shoulder. "Granted."

Side note: Considering how Inferno just released his golden ass from prison, you'd think Lucifer would be a little nicer. *What a dick.*

"These three are lying to you" says Inferno. "She is both Xavier's daughter and the Great Scala. The man walking Obsidian over is her husband and King of the Thrax. Obsidian does not serve them; he's been waiting in Black Wing Manor for two thousand years, watching over your prison."

Lucifer pulls his golden sword from its sheath. "Then I'll kill them all after I cut down the ghoul."

Kill us all? That's harsh. At least, Happy and Jaime have slipped off while all this went down. If nothing else, they'll survive. That's a comfort.

On second thought, a comfort would be Walker taking down Captain Entitlement here. And I know just how to help him do it.

"Get on with it," orders Lucifer.

Lincoln guides a very freaked-out looking Obsidian over to my side.

"What is this?" hisses Obsidian under his breath.

"Here's the deal," I say. "Do you know magnifying spells?"

"What?"

"They're often called accelerators," says Lincoln.

"Yes, I do."

"When I put this healing mojo into Walker, I want you to put in an accelerator spell too. That way, when Lucifer hits him …" I pause, giving Obsidian a chance to catch on. It seems like he needs a moment.

"… Walker will grow stronger, not weaker," finishes Obsidian. "The magic won't last long, though."

I shoot him a dry look. "Like that's the worst part of this plan."

Walker gives me a weak smile. "Hey, I love this idea."

To Obsidian's credit, now that he has the plan down, he jumps right in. Lowering his head, the seraphim murmurs an incantation. Soon his staff comes to life. The raven head carving opens its beak. Thin tendrils of red power reach out to encircle Walker.

After dropping the canopic jar, I smash it open with my boot. Once again, threads of blue power rise from the shattered container. I scoop the energy into my hands and press it into Walker's chest.

Instantly, the wounds on Walker's skin close over and heal. His color returns to its regular deathly pale. The remainder of Obsidian's spell enters Walker as well.

"You look ready." Lucifer swoops his blade down. No question where Inferno learned her love of beheadings. Lucifer goes right for the neck.

Walker crouches low, dodging the attack. I slip my baculum into his hands.

What a total scumbag move from Lucifer, by the way. Dad told me about archangel challenges. They should begin with an official listing of the rules. After that, there's a spell that holds everyone to those rules. Plus, Walker's naked from the waist up and Lucifer is in full body armor. *Cheap shot.*

Walker takes a pointed step further out of the range of Lucifer's blade. "I thought this was an official challenge," states Walker. "Aren't you supposed to read the rules before you attack?"

"Rules are for archangels."

"Then renounce this challenge. Retreat from fighting a ghoul." Walker tilts his head, his all-black eyes fixed on Lucifer.

Long seconds pass before Lucifer speaks again. "I choose to fight you. We shall begin by listing the official rules for the challenge. No magical weapons." In a supreme act of dick-i-tude, Lucifer swipes his blade at Walker's neck again.

Walker ignites my baculum as a long sword, spins about and meets Lucifer's strike. Sparks of angel fire erupt where their weapons meet. "How about this weapon?" asks Walker smoothly. "Acceptable?"

Now, my father told me all about archangel challenges. Trying to kill your opponent while reading the rules is not okay.

For a fraction of a second, Lucifer's eyes widen. He wasn't expecting Walker to counter his strike. *Good.* If I know Walker —*and I do*—then Lucifer isn't expecting a lot of things.

Lucifer leans in closer to Walker. The archangel places more pressure on where their swords meet, trying to force Walker into stumbling away. It doesn't work. Fresh arcs of power and light pour off from the spot where their blades clash.

"Your weapon is acceptable. Next rule. No magic spells once the battle starts."

"But I heal. It's my gift from Aquila. I can hide the look of the healing taking place. However, the magic itself is part of my soul."

More sparks appear than ever before. Lucifer leans in even closer. His eyes narrow. "Then have your mages block the power."

"No. Retreat from the challenge."

The barest flicker of muscle appears in Walker's neck. I know my honorary brother well enough to realize this point about healing is important.

Lucifer simply must agree.

But Lucifer doesn't say a word. Instead, the archangel launches into a series of classic strikes. His golden blade swoops in high. Or goes low to take out Walker at the hip or knees. I've seen this tactic. Lucifer's testing Walker's skills. And being a creep who won't finish reading the freaking rules.

I cough, and it sounds a lot like *'cheater, cheater.'*

Walker meets every assault. My heart soars. I keep shooting Walker thumbs-up, even though I doubt he can see it. That's what he did for me.

There's another pause when their blades lock.

"Your assistants cast spells before," says Lucifer. "The magic was for accelerated healing. That won't save you in the end, but it makes this battle more interesting. I accept the challenge and allow your power to heal."

Now it's Walker's turn to have his eyes widen a fraction. I must admit, I'm shocked as well. I thought Lucifer was spending all his time being a self-righteous dick. I had no idea he was watching what Obsidian and I were doing.

"Agreed," says Walker. "Cast the spell to bind our actions to the rules."

Now, there's supposed to be a formal binding spell ceremony. In a surprise move, Lucifer skips that. With their blades still locked, Lucifer speaks.

"I hereby launch the archangels' duel. No magic other than what we've agreed. No weapons other than what we carry. No outside help."

At these words, I shoot a glance in Inferno's direction. Sure enough, she's scowling. Tough. No saving your boss, lady.

"The duel ends when one of us is dead." Lucifer grins. He so thinks he's going to kill Walker. "And only an archangel can kill another archangel."

Golden light flares out from Lucifer's body, encasing both the King of the Angels and Walker in brightness. Energy and power zing through the air. A moment later, the golden light is gone.

The binding spell is cast.

Lucifer launches another barrage of strikes. His blade moves so quickly, the movements are hard to follow. Walker meets every assault. Bands of worry tighten around my rib cage. Meeting attack volleys is not enough. For Walker to win, he must get on the offensive.

Walker launches into a series of aggressive leaps and thrusts. His baculum blade slams into Lucifer's golden weapon, over and over. At one point, Walker strikes Lucifer's armor at the shoulder. Lines of spark and fire speed out from the spot.

Lucifer counterattacks. His moves become so fast, everything becomes a blur. During one strike, Lucifer's blade grazes Walker's shoulder.

White light bursts from the wound. The cut closes up.

Lucifer gapes at the spot. "What was that?"

"Aquila said the same thing once," replies Walker. "When it became clear I inherited her gift for healing, she taught me how to hide the light."

Lincoln and I share a shocked look. "Did you know light comes out of Walker's wounds and he somehow hides it?" After all, I've seen Walker fight tons of times. I've never seen this before.

"I did not."

Whoa. My honorary older brother holds so many secrets, I wonder how he keeps track of them all. If he's been concealing this light-thing, then that must have a purpose.

Next, Walker does the last thing I'd ever expect. He extinguishes his baculum. The move is so shocking, I'm stunned into silence. And for me, that takes a lot. Walker raises his arms out to the side. The stance makes one fact clear. Walker is helpless.

Or maybe not.

The way Walker keeps glaring at Lucifer, it's more of a challenge than anything.

Strike me.

Lucifer doesn't waste any time. Raising his arm, Lucifer brings down his golden sword and skewers Walker through the chest.

For a moment, my world shatters. Walker stands before me, a golden sword piercing his sternum. Even ghouls can die from wounds like that. It's a reflex more than anything, but I start to race toward my honorary brother. Lincoln grips my elbow, holding me back.

"Wait," my guy whispers in my ear. "Walker might be fine."

Lucifer pulls his blade out from Walker's chest. But unlike Trav, Walker doesn't fall to the ground. Instead, white light pours from his chest wound. Walker's skin turns from deathly pale to something resembling alive.

Walker is healing. Transforming. *But into what?*

"This is my battle," roars Lucifer. "You go down."

Swinging his blade, Lucifer pierces Walker again and again. The King of Angels strikes Walker through the shoulder, liver, you name it. Each wound lights up until Walker's flesh heals and transforms. Soon golden light flares out from his skin. More brightness arches behind him until something appears.

Wings.

And Walker gains not just any wings, but golden wings. The sign of an archangel.

Lucifer pauses, stunned. "What is this?"

"My healing power comes from Aquila, not my ghoul side. So each time you hurt me, I revive as a little more archangel."

A strange kind of light shines in Lucifer's eyes. It's like he's putting together some kind of puzzle he hadn't detected before.

"It's you?" asks the King of the Angels.

"Yes," replies Walker. "It's me."

Now I'm not sure what *that* little exchange really meant, but it was certainly a big deal. Unfortunately, knowing my honorary brother, it might be ages before I discover the secret behind all this. That said, I know one thing. Only and archangel can kill another archangel, and Walker now has golden wings.

This is getting good.

"You caused the deaths of millions," declares Walker. "Now I'm putting you back in your cage."

Then Walker, all glowing skin and massive golden wings, grabs Lucifer like the guy's made of tissue paper. Walker tosses the archangel into the air, bringing Lucifer down so the archangels torso snaps down over Walker's knee. Lucifer's golden armor crumples under the impact.

My brows lift. That was one of the most classic moves in the history of cheesy wresting. And it was awesome.

Rising, Walker punches Lucifer straight in the face. Over and over. Blood streams down the archangel's chin and flecks his golden hair. Walker steps back. For a second, Lucifer stands perfectly still.

Then the King of the Angels falls over in a heap.

"No!" Inferno spreads her wings and flies right at Walker. Inferno's sword is out and she's ready to kill. Walker waits until the lava angel is within striking range. Then my honorary brother punches Inferno once in the face, hard. She drops like a stone.

Whoa.

Note to self: never piss off Walker.

Leaning over, Walker grabs Lucifer's ankle, then Inferno's, and starts dragging them both into Black Wing Manor. Throughout the whole deal, Inferno and Lucifer stay totally unconscious. The two don't even notice their heads thunking against the steps as Walker drags them up the stairs.

My honorary brother pauses by the front door. "Are you all coming?"

It takes me a moment for my brain to start working again. Walker kicked Lucifer's ass and then Inferno's. Now, he's dragging them both around by the ankle.

Love this.

"Oh, we're joining you all right," I look to Obsidian. "How about you?"

"Of course."

"Count me in as well." Lincoln gestures toward the passed-out Lucifer and Inferno. "Do you need help with that?"

"Nope." Walker trudges through the front door. Lucifer and Inferno's skulls smash into the frame as he drags them along. "I've got it."

And so he does. Damn.

CHAPTER 28

*M*inutes later, our group steps into the manor's underground prison chamber. Walker drops Lucifer and Inferno off by the doorway, literally. The low boulder that covered the labyrinth's entrance has since been moved away. Drayden's no longer connected to the stone, either. Walker's brother lays crumpled in a corner, his skin a deathly shade of gray.

Walker races to Drayden's side. "Brother. It's me."

Drayden opens his eyes a crack. "Walker." His head reaches up. "Wings."

"Yes, Drayden." Walker's voice shakes. "I have wings."

All this time, Lincoln, Obsidian, and I wait by the entrance. Seeing Walker and his brother together warms my soul. And the archangel wing-thing? Dad will love it. I take Lincoln's hand in mine. "Isn't this awesome?"

My husband forces the smallest of grins. "Yes."

I scrunch my brows together in confusion. Walker and Drayden's reunion is so sweet. And the archangel wings are beyond awesome. But for some reason, Lincoln's acting bummed out. *What's wrong?*

A chill of memory moves up my neck. *Crud.* I'd been so exited to see Walker kick ass and drag those two creeps around, I forgot about why we're here.

Lucifer must return to his prison.

Inferno's probably going in, too.

Then someone must take Drayden's place as Labyrinth Master.

That someone is supposed to be Walker.

My heart sinks. *No, not this.*

Stepping away from Drayden, Walker stomps over to the still-unconscious Lucifer. Grabbing the archangel by the ankle, Walker unceremoniously spins the guy across the very-dusty floor, sending the King of Angels flying down into the dungeon entrance like an archangel *hole in one*. Grabbing Inferno's ankle, Walker does the same with her. There's a long wait before there's the thud of bodies hitting the floor below. I'd wonder if those two are all right, but I've fought big bads my entire life.

Ones like Lucifer and Inferno always end up fine.

Walker steps to the far side of the low boulder. Pressing his palms against the rock, Walker pushes the massive stone across the floor with ease. There's the sound of crunching rock and a few puffs of dust. Soon, the low boulder covers the Labyrinth entrance once more. His work done, Walker brushes off his hands. With a glow of light, his wings disappear from his back.

I check my watch. Only seven minutes left.

Seven minutes before Walker is magically sealed in as Labyrinth Master. It's on the tip of my tongue to ask if we can heal Drayden and put him back as Labyrinth Master, but I know my Walker. Drayden just had the job for two thousand years. There's no way Walker will allow his brother to return to that rock.

No, Walker will be the next Labyrinth Master.

I try to accept this fate.

Nope, not happening.

"I've got an idea," I announce. "How about you pull back that rock, haul out Lucifer, and kill him? The guy is a waste of angelic space."

Walker sighs. "If I could have, I would have. I'm not 100% pure archangel yet. And if Lucifer and I fight again, he's watched my every move. Tracked my style. The victory won't be easy or even assured." Walker points at maze below our feet. "This is our chance to get Lucifer back into prison and keep the after-realms safe."

Maybe. But Walker stuck on a rock? No way. My mind reels through options and possibilities. Sadly, I keep coming up empty.

Lincoln takes my hands in his. "What do you have for us?"

My voice cracks. "Nothing."

"No, Myla. I know you. I've seen your strength and soul. This is the same as Lucifer's Gauntlets and the gate. There's a solution here. You'll find it."

A shock of inspiration corkscrews up my spine. I suck in a shaky breath. *Lucifer's Gauntlets.* In all the excitement, I forgot I was still wearing them. Looking down, I glance at the watch.

We still have six minutes.

A plan forms in my mind.

"So." Lincoln gives my hands a squeeze. "What do you have for us now?"

"Lucifer's Gauntlets, a watch, and a freaky idea."

"What can I say?" Lincoln grins. "I love this plan."

I round on Obsidian. "You built this prison, right?"

"With the other seraphim."

Peeling off my watch, I hand it to Obsidian. "There was an identical version of this watch with all sorts of spells loaded on it. Here's what I need to know. If I pull out Drayden's magical intellect out with these gauntlets, can you place that power in this watch? Then you magically slap the souped-up watch on the big-ass rock and bing-bang-boom, no more need for a Labyrinth Master."

Obsidian turns the device over in his palm. "It can attempt it, certainly. No one's done anything like this before."

I make my hand into a puppet-shape and have it talk. "*Blah blah blah* no one's done it before. You're awesome. You've got this."

True, the *hand puppet thing* is is not my most mature moment, but this idea might save Walker. What can I say? I get a little over-excited sometimes.

Walker frowns. "I don't like the idea of removing Drayden's magical brilliance."

"We'll repair Drayden's mind later on, easy peasy. Here's how it will work. You put more Walker-style healing power into a new canopic jar, then I'll set that mojo into Drayden with my gauntlets." I twiddle my fingers as demonstration. "Drayden's mind will be healed. His magical genius will return."

"Really, Myla?" Walker glares at me. He so knows I'm fibbing here because I don't want him plastered to a rock forever.

"Actually," I say. "He'll be mostly fine."

More glaring. "Myla."

"Okay, maybe quite possibly he'll be totally fine."

Super glaring. "Maybe."

"Honestly, I have no idea if that will work."

Drayden slowly shifts into a seated position. "I refuse for Walker to become Labyrinth Master just so I can keep my intellect. I accept the risk that healing energy might not repair me."

"So, it's agreed?" I ask.

Walker still isn't bought in. "You've never done this without a canopic jar. How do you know you can even pull out Drayden's magical intellect?"

Rounding on Walker, I set my fist on my hip. "Do you really think you'll stop me here?"

My honorary brother tries the *glaring thing* again. This time, it fails miserably. "No, I've never talked you out of anything."

"Precisely." Marching over to Drayden, I kneel by his side. "I hope this won't hurt."

Drayden fixes me with his all-black eyes. "I'm ready."

Reaching forward, I set my fingertips on Drayden's forehead. When I used the canopic jars, I said: *'Raise the angels! Awaken!'* Some kind of magical command is probably needed here as well.

"Release his brilliance," I say in a low voice.

For a long moment, nothing happens. Then threads of blue light slowly wind out from Drayden's forehead. I grip the magic cords with my gauntlets. My heart pounds with such strength, my pulse beats in my throat.

"Got some magic blue stuff here," I announce. "How's it coming with the watch?"

From behind me, I hear Obsidian's low murmur, followed by the caw of his bird staff. I could turn around and see what the seraphim is up to, but I'm holding a bunch of blue brain magic in my hands. No way do I want to drop it.

Obsidian's footsteps sound as he approaches me from behind. He kneels beside me. A moment later, Obsidian sets his hand beside mine. The watch sits on his palm.

Good.

And it glows red with seraphim power.

Even better.

My stomach tumbles.

Please, let this work.

My head gets all fuzzy from excitement and terror. Walker's life is on the line. Things get hard to follow. I'm pretty sure Obsidian murmurs more magic stuff. Maybe his bird staff thingy caws a few more times. At some point, Obsidian must have asked me to put Drayden blue brain threads into the watch, because before I know it, Lincoln's at my side.

"There's no need to worry," says Lincoln calmly to Obsidian. "I'll help her finish."

With gentle movements, Lincoln guides my hands so I place

the magic threads atop the watch. The thin cords of light wriggle their way inside the device. Azure brilliance bursts from the watch.

I scan Obsidian's face. *Did it work?*

Beside us, the flat boulder starts to shimmy.

Thud! Thud! Thud!

Someone's hitting the stone from underneath.

One guess who.

As if we needed clarity, Lucifer and Inferno's muffled voices sound from under the stone, saying comforting things like *'You'll die for this!'* and *'We'll peel you like a pear!'*

After marches over to the boulder, Obsidian slams the base of his staff onto the rock. He calls out a fresh set of spells, still in that strange language. Red tendrils of power wind off his staff. The raven's head comes alive, caws, and then wriggles its way free from the staff itself.

Huh. I had no idea it could do that.

Taking to wing, the raven plucks the watch face from Obsidian's palm. Somewhere along the line, Obsidian removed the band. The bird circles over the stone as the boulder shifts due to more hits from below. Lucifer and Inferno sound again.

"We'll hunt you down!"

"You'll plead for death!"

The bird keeps circling the stone. My fingers itch to grab the thing and slap it on the rock where it belongs. Doesn't Obsidian see that Lucifer and Inferno are about to break free?

At last, the bird circles down and lands atop the stone. It pecks at the watch. With each touch, the device sets deeper into the rock.

Then the massive stone comes to life.

The boulder lights up. Shifting patterns of labyrinth lines appear on its surface. A long howl sounds as Lucifer and Inferno fall away from the stone to get trapped somewhere deep in the labyrinth. Obsidian crosses the room to heal Drayden.

It worked. Walker does not have to be Labyrinth Master.

With that, I've officially had it. In general, I'm not the type of girl who partakes of spontaneous swoons. In fact, I've never had one before. Yet white lights are definitely spotting my vision. My legs become all gooey beneath me. I turn to Lincoln.

"I think I'm passing ou—"

My guy scoops me into his arms. "I've got you."

And so I'm smiling while everything around me vanishes into darkness.

*L*incoln and I step up the gravel path to Black Wing Manor. There's still a ton of fog all around, but now Jaime has placed small lanterns on either side of the walkway, so people won't fall while approaching front door.

Jaime is thoughtful like that.

I grip the small gift box against my chest. "Do you think this is right?"

Lincoln gives me the side eye. "What, the Elvis T-shirt is too much?"

Now that Lincoln is King of the Thrax, he's switched out all his *Purple Rain* tour stuff for Elvis. Tonight he's wearing low-slung blue jeans and funky black shoes as well as an *Viva Las Vegas* T-shirt. I'm in black jeans with a ruffled top and heels. Actual heels. It will be a miracle if I get through tonight without snapping a vertebrae.

I tap the gift box. "No, I mean the present. What's appropriate to get seraphim and thrax as a house warming gift? I have no idea."

"They just want to have people around and celebrate. It'll be fine." Lincoln coughs and it sounds a lot like *'Walker wrapped it.'*

My eyes almost bug out of my head. Walker can be a bit of prankster under regular circumstances, but now that his brother Drayden is back and healthy? The ghoul's positively unhinged. I thought once the two of them reunited, Walker and Drayden would stroll about acting noble. Help old ladies with their laundry, save kittens from trees, that kind of thing. Instead, they've been like two nine year olds on a goof-off bender.

Oh, well. I guess they deserve it.

But now I wonder what Walker did with the gift box.

We march up the steps to the front door. Jaime whips it open before there's even a chance to knock. The guy looks positively blissed out. He's also a little more dressy than before with his skinny jeans, a button down, and actual product in his hair. Dating Obsidian definitely agrees with the guy.

"Myla! Lincoln! You're here!"

On a side note, I'm so pleased that Jaime has dropped the whole *Your Highness* thing. It's nice to have another buddy.

"We wouldn't miss it," says Lincoln.

Jaime wraps us in deep hugs. Once he's done, he sets a hand on our shoulders. "No one knows about *you know what*, right?"

Jaime asks us this every time we see him. The official word is that the seraphim haven't been dead all this time. They've just been giving proper burials to the entire Brimstone Legion. And it's not a total lie. It did take the seraphim a while to hide all the stone angels. Oh, and the official word also incudes saying that the battle turned the seraphim all into steam punk guys made of metal. Surprisingly enough, people are buying it. Even Dad. I mean, we're not inviting my father over to tour Black Wing Manor or anything, but it's all gone down pretty smoothly.

"Don't worry," I say. "Dad still doesn't suspect a thing. Neither to do the other archangels. It was a genius idea to have the seraphim spontaneously visit them all."

A dreamy look settles on Jaime's face. "That was Sid's idea."

Speaking of the seraphim, Obsidian appears at Jaime's side

and swings the door open wide. Talk about a transformation. Obsidian is rocking this dark tunic thing with loose pants. It says *'I'm a badass modern magic user.'* He still wears his long hair tied back as well as a huge smile on his handsome face. "Welcome!"

I push forward the box. "We brought napkin rings."

Okay, maybe I should have saved the rings for another moment. But I don't do parties. In high school, I was too busy killing things and being a social pariah. Any parties consisted of me and Cissy hanging out, so there wasn't a formal rhythm to what happened.

If I missed some kind of social cue, Jaime doesn't show it. "Wonderful!" The thrax beams with excitement as he rips the box open. Then, he frowns.

Obsidian reaches across to pull out a stack of papers from the box. He reads the top one. "This says: *Coupon for Obsidian. Good for one hug.*" He flips to the next sheet. "*Coupon for Jaime. Good for one chore.*" And the next. "*Coupon for Jaime. Good for one day without raven shit.*"

Jaime swipes that one from Obsidian's hand. "I'm keeping this one."

I risk a look at Lincoln. My guy's face is red from trying to hold in laughter. That's when I put it together.

Walker.

"I'll take these." I scoop the remaining coupons from Obsidian. "Walker did this. It's his idea of a joke."

Obsidian smiles again. "Whatever makes Walker happy."

Jaime pokes through the rest of the box. "I love them!"

"They're silver and have the crest of the House of Rixa."

Obsidian picks one up. "Which is an Eagle." He frowns. "Those attack ravens."

"Only when called for," says Jaime with a wink. "They're perfect. We need more thrax-inspired stuff around here." Jaime loops his arm with Obsidian's. Together they step backward.

"Come on in. Say hello. People here have been dying to meet you."

We say our thanks and start working the crowd. The interior of the house is still dark wood and raven carvings, but Jaime has added a ton more light fixtures and some paintings. The place feels much more homey and comfortable. And based on the number of people hanging out, I'm not the only one who thinks so.

Across the crowd, I spy Cissy and Zeke. My bestie was beyond thrilled when she got the invitation to this house warming. Ciss believes this is a great chance to build diplomatic bridges with the Dark Lands. And if anyone can manage that articular feat, it'll be Ciss. Spotting me, she gives a wink. My bestie is in a deep discussion with a ghoul ambassador, so I plan to catch up with her later.

Lincoln and I don't step far into the house when Happy races up to us. She wears a yellow bustle gown for the occasion as well as a wide grin. *Dazzling.*

"Hey there!" cries Happy. "I want you to meet my parents!"

Grabbing our wrists, Happy guides me and Lincoln over to a man and woman who are also dressed from the 1800's. Happy's father is dapper with his high-breasted coat and bowler hat. Her mother wears a yellow gown that matches Happy's. They all have the same ebony skin, mismatched eyes, and excited vibe.

"We're so pleased to meet you," says Happy's father. "I'm Leo."

"I'm Prudence," says Happy's mom. "Our daughter told us not to address you formally. I hope that's acceptable."

"It's perfect," I say. And I mean it. This is like my first normal party with regular people, meaning they are mostly *not* in medieval garb. Plus, no one's treating me like a queen or Great Scala. I'm having the time of my life.

"We can't thank you enough for all you've done," says Leo. "There's a new Chosen One every two hundred years or so. It's unusual for one so young to be sent to Black Wing Manor, but the Viper had been breaking in. Obsidian needed extra help."

"Plus," adds Prudence. "Happy isn't a typical girl. And we knew she had Jaime to watch over her." She sighs. "I wish we could have stayed here as well."

"Trust me, Mom. You wouldn't have liked it."

I raise my hand. "I'll vouch there."

We then have a lovely conversation, mostly discussing ideas for incorporating the true mission of the House of Victoriana into official thrax life. The whole Lucifer prison aspect will stay a secret, but it's important that Victoriana enhances our alliance with the Dark Lands. If this experience has taught us anything, it's that we all need better bridges between our various realms.

Eventually, we leave Happy and find the cookie table area. Walker approaches. Tonight, he's in his artist get-up of jeans and a paint-splattered T-shirt. "Hello, uh, Myla. Lincoln. How are you?"

I try to talk through a mouthful of cookie. "Fine. Where's Drayden?"

"I need to talk to you about him," says Walker. "It's very serious."

Lincoln leans against the table, an unreadable look on his face. "What is it?"

"Did he lose his magical intellect?" I ask. "I put your healing mojo in his head, just like we planned. He's been fine ever since. Super smart and everything."

"It's not that," replies Walker. "Drayden's genius is still intact."

My insides twist with worry. "Then what is it?"

Walker lets out a dramatic sigh. "Myla, Drayden's in love with you. He created this little shrine to you in the bathroom and everything. I don't know what to do."

My mouth falls open. Bits of cookie tumble to the floor. "What?"

Walker points right at my nose. "Got you!" He swipes his hand over his cheek and head, revealing that the classic Walker hair-style of sideburns and a brush cut was just drawn on. This isn't Walker. It's Drayden.

I groan. "Good one. You totally got me."

Walker steps out from the shadows. He's wearing the same outfit as Drayden. Both start laughing their asses off. The real Walker points at my nose. "You should have seen your face!"

"Ha, ha."

It takes ten minutes for Walker and Drayden to move on from the topic of their awesome prank. But it does happen. Soon we launch into a chat that ranges from our favorite new painters to the best old battle tactics. The conversation eventually veers onto Armageddon.

Drayden shakes his head. "I can't believe he turned out to be such a terrible character. Last I heard, he was just a common demon."

So that segues to a long retelling of all the Armageddon adventures. Drayden seems suitably astonished. I assure him that after our last close encounter with Armageddon and Lucifer's Coin, that the King of Hell is officially out of chances to escape and ruin our lives. There's no way we'll hear from that guy again. *Hopefully.*

Next Drayden shares his plans for a multi-year world tour. Afterwards, I pull Walker aside and push him about the archangel stuff. My honorary brother shuts me down every time. Walker wants his archangel nature kept a secret. He won't even show his wings anymore. According to Walker, the world must see him as a ghoul, period. And no, I still can't tell Mom and Dad.

Whatever. I'll get the truth out of Walker eventually. I always do.

Lincoln steps up and reminds me we have an early morning appointment. I need my rest. Sadly, that means we have to leave.

We make our goodbyes and head back to Purgatory. This is one appointment that I don't want to miss.

CHAPTER 30

a few hours later, Lincoln and I wait offstage at the set of *Good Morning Purgatory*. This time, I'm totally awake and alert. I didn't even drool on Lincoln's suit.

A short distance away, Becky Tizzle speaks to the camera. "Next up, we have the Great Scala and her Consort! Let's give them a big round of applause!"

Lincoln and I walk on stage and take our classic positions on the love seat across from Becky.

The host pulls up a clipboard. "You both ran off on me last time. Very naughty! I have a long list of questions for you."

Lincoln leans forward. "Myla and I promised to report back on the Viper. So we've returned with an exclusive round up of how this fiend was captured and killed."

The audience gasps.

Becky almost falls out of her seat. "Tell me you have video."

"We do," I say. "Roll it, Fred."

What follows next is a mostly true telling about the Enmity brothers. We cover how they found Lucifer's Gauntlets, turned to a life of crime (that's the true stuff) and eventually died during a shoot out at their farm (and that's the not so true part.) We include lots of magically created video that shows Zeke bravely leading the charge at the farm shootout. We also share updated video on the recovery of the Viper Brothers' victims. By using Lucifer's Gauntlets and Walker's ability to heal, everyone's had their original demonic abilities returned.

And so it goes. Becky asks lots of questions. We answer with as few lies as possible. My tail makes periodic waves to the audience for attention. That always gets a big laugh.

"Well," says Becky at length. "That was an amazing exclusive. The President of Purgatory will be on our show later today for a mayor's conference recap. Will she have any comments about the Viper Brothers?"

"She will," I reply. "My mother will also provide instructions for how to properly handle unknown magical items. Lucifer's Gauntlets are now safely stored in Heaven. If the Enmity Brothers had reported them right away, all this could have been avoided."

"Thank you so much, Great Scala and Consort." Becky turns to the screen. "And now, we have a real treat for you. A surprise guest!"

I grab Lincoln's had. We both know who the surprise guest is here. I fight the urge to bounce up and down on the loveseat.

"We're starting a new segment on supernatural child rearing," announces Becky. "And here's our guest host, Xavier, Purgatory's First Man!"

Dad walks out on set wearing jeans, a button-down, and a massive backpack that holds baby Maxon. Lincoln and I stand up, give them hugs, and let Dad take the stage. Lincoln and I step off camera, where Mom waits in her purple suit. She's smiling her face off. "I'm so proud of Xavier. I'm so proud of you two. Hell, I'm proud of everyone!"

Back on stage, Becky blushes up a storm. I forget how most women find my father crazy-handsome. "Would you like to sit, Xavier?" asks Becky.

"Easier if I stand," explains Dad. He points behind him, as evidence of why vertical is the best position. For his part, Maxon pops his cherub head over Dad's shoulder, gives a gummy grin, and says: "Pop pops."

I blink back tears while Dad pulls a few crackers and hands them to Maxon. My son chows down while my father talks.

"Today, I'm going to discuss the importance of scheduling with child rearing."

"And why are schedules so critical?" asks Becky.

"You have to find a balance. Too much detail, you lose the child. No context or structure, and you can have a tantrum on your hands. Roll the tape, Fred."

The show cuts over to various videos of Dad and Maxon. Reading books. Eating lunch. Tickling.

"What do you think?" Mom whispers.

"Xavier's doing a phenomenal job," replies Lincoln. "No one would guess he was struggling just a month ago."

Mom lowers her voice. "To tell the truth, I knew I'd be called away to the mayor's conference. When it comes to kids, sometimes you just have to jump in."

We all return our attention to Dad's presentation. He's segued onto his top ten nutrition tips. Maxon has taken to gumming his hand. Suddenly, Mom's previous advice about Dad comes back to me in bright red letters. Sometimes, you have to savor a beautiful moment.

I slip up beside Lincoln, rest my head on his shoulder, and enjoy.

—*The End*—
The adventure continues with THE BRUTAL TIME,
Book 6 in the Angelbound Origins Series

NEXT IN ANGELBOUND SERIES – THE BRUTAL TIME

Don't miss THE BRUTAL TIME, Book 6 in the Angelbound Origins Series.

ANGELBOUND LINCOLN

Experience the events of ANGELBOUND from Prince Lincoln's point of view!

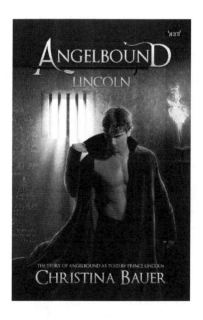

CHRISTINA BAUER'S MAGICORUM

Modern fairy tales with sass, action, and romance.

CHRISTINA BAUER'S DIMENSION
DRIFT

A dystopian adventure with science, snark, and hot aliens.

CHRISTINA BAUER'S BEHOLDER

A medieval farm girl finds necromancy and love.

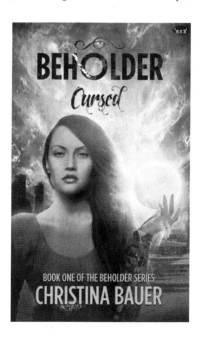

IF YOU ENJOYED THIS BOOK…

…Please consider leaving a review, even if it's just a line or two. Every bit truly helps, especially for those of us who don't *write by the numbers,* if you know what I mean. Plus I have it on good authority that every time you review an indie author, somewhere an angel gets a mocha latte. For reals.

And angels need their caffeine, too.

ACKNOWLEDGMENTS

Gulp.

Double gulp.

I'm taking the plunge and have decided to become an author full time.

Yipes!

Did I mention that I'm freaking out? Well, I am.

Here's the story on my full time fears. On the next few pages, you'll see the somewhat insane list of books that have been lurking in my brain and can now get OUT OF MY FUCKING HEAD over the next few years. I'm told it's too aggressive and might overwhelm you, my dear readership.

Eep.

Still, I can't help it. Stories churn around my soul. If don't release them in time, I worry they'll evaporate into the ethos. Besides, my internal reality is really fractured. It helps to share it with others who go: *wow, that's kind of cool!*

So there you have it. Thanks in advance for your support and understanding, because I'll definitely do something stupid as I make this journey. But no matter what turns this path may take,

I'd like to commence by showing my appreciation to the team of crazies who've helped make this all possible.

First, there is the amazing team at Inscribe Digital. They believed in me and my vision from the start. Thank you, Kelly Peterson, Ana Szaky, Katy Beehler, and Allison Davis. You're marvels!!!

Next, there's the wonderful team at Monster House Books. Arely Zimmermann, where would I be without you? I shiver to even think about. Plus, I'm incredibly proud to see you grow as a businesswoman and editor.

And I can never forget you, my dear readers and bloggers. You guys are the best, end of story. Thank you for every high five, sweet idea, and suggested change. Mwah!

Most importantly, my deepest appreciation goes out to my husband and son. Your patience and support mean everything. I love you both with all my heart and soul.

COLLECTED WORKS

Angelbound Worlds

Inside stories about your fav characters

1. Xavier (Spring 2020)
2. Cissy (Spring 2021)

Beholder

A medieval farm girl discovers necromancy and love

1. Cursed
2. Concealed
3. Cherished
4. Crowned
5. Cradled

Fairy Tales of the Magicorum

Modern fairy tales with sass, action, and romance

1. Wolves and Roses
1.5 Moonlight and Midtown
2. Shifters and Glyphs
3. Slippers and Thieves (Fall 2019)
4. Bandits and Ballgowns (Fall 2020)

Dimension Drift

A dystopian future with science, snark, and hot aliens

Prequels

1. Scythe
2. Umbra

Novels

1. Alien Minds (Spring 2019)
2. ECHO Academy (Spring 2020)
3. Drift Warrior (Spring 2021)

Publisher's Note: Christina Bauer is a non-linear thinker who came up with ARMAGEDDON and then went back and wrote some earlier books. This is why you'll see ARMAGEDDON (Book 7) and the Offspring series available before THE BRUTAL TIME (Book 6). We've told her to stop this practice, but she keeps giving us lewd hand gestures in response. Apologies in advance for any inconvenience.

ABOUT CHRISTINA BAUER

Christina Bauer thinks that fantasy books are like bacon: they just make life better. All of which is why she writes romance novels that feature demons, dragons, wizards, witches, elves, elementals, and a bunch of random stuff that she brainstorms while riding the Boston T. Oh, and she includes lots of humor and kick-ass chicks, too. Christina lives in Newton, MA with her husband, son, and semi-insane golden retriever, Ruby.

Stalk Christina on Social Media – She Loves It!

Blog: http://monsterhousebooks.com/blog/category/christina

Facebook: https://www.facebook.com/authorBauer/

Twitter: @CB_Bauer

Instagram: https://www.instagram.com/christina_cb_bauer/

Web site: www.bauersbooks.com

AUTHOR NOTE

Welcome to the last bit of the book! Since we're both hanging here, I'll share some behind-the-scenes facts about THE DARK LANDS.

The character of Jaime is inspired by Jane of *Jane Eyre*, aka one of the classics of Gothic-ness. From the same book, Obsidian is a version of Mister Rochester, only instead of (SPOILER ALERT!) an insane wife in the attic, Obsidian endures having all his brothers and sisters frozen outside. IMHO, Obsidian has the harder deal. And I ship Jaime and Obsidian far more than Jane and Rochester. But then again, I may have an teensy bias.

In keeping with the *Jane Eyre* theme, Happy is a re-imagining of Jane's student, Adèle. I always thought that Adèle got a little shafted in terms of character development when it came to being fierce. Let's be honest; that girl was a dingbat. So I had fun making Happy both smart and badass.

There's also a lot of Edgar Allen Poe in here. Why? I was a wee bit obsessed with Poe as a teenager. Hence the ravens. So many ravens. I tried to have heartbeats in the floor or bury someone in the wall. The closest to got was slapping the Labyrinth Master to a rock. Thank you, EA Poe.

In general, I had a freaking blast writing this book. I hope that shines through on the page! Creating the scenes with Xavier and Maxon was especially fun. Everything was based on my actual experiences as a parent, and it was a joy to relive-slash-share those memories.

On a final note, I'm thrilled to more fully introduce the villain of Lucifer, as well as his not-yet-defined relationship with Walker. I've had this stuff outlined since Angelbound Book 1, and it's beyond awesome to start that journey with you.

I look forward to seeing you again at THE BRUTAL TIME (Angelbound Origins Book 6). Happy reading!

-Christina